Getti

Getting A Life

Samantha Rugen

Piccadilly Press • London

Printed and bound by Progressive Printing Ltd, Leigh-on-Sea
for the publishers Piccadilly Press Ltd.,
5 Castle Road, London NW1 8PR

A catalogue record for this book is available from the British
Library

ISBN: 1 85340 314 8 (hardback)
1 85340 319 9 (trade paperback)

Samantha Rugen is a young Liverpudlian illustrator. She also
works as a primary school teacher. Piccadilly Press also
published her first book: *Everything A Girl Should Know.*

Introduction

Dear Reader,

Please allow me to introduce myself. My name is Jane, a boring name, which I recently decided to do something about. I knew I couldn't change it to anything too unusual and exciting, like Destiny or Atlanta, without a lot of hassle. However, I added a bit of spice to it by putting in a 'y', thus changing it to Jayne, rather than Janey.

My surname is slightly more interesting. It's Schwartzkopf. I was really proud of it until we had our first ever German lesson and we had to introduce ourselves to the class. The teacher was kind enough to use my name as an example to translate, and promptly made me one of the biggest jokes of the year. Schwartzkopf means 'black head'. Never has my skin been so closely scrutinised by so many! Thankfully, someone stole my thunder and attention was paid to a new girl unfortunately burdened with the name of Mitzy Macmanus. From then on both German and non-German speaking pupils could enjoy her name together.

I think all that name-calling caused some kind of turning point in my life. Things seemed to go downhill from then on. Paranoia, depression, boredom, fluffiness, spottiness and fatness were thrown at me in a frenzied fashion as puberty hit me with great speed. Add all that to the problems you are about to read about, which include my best friend, Em, moving away, and it seemed a pretty bad start to a new school year. But things weren't all bad. I had Meg and Dave to keep me company.

I do have the occasional disagreement with Meg and I admit this is partly because I'm jealous of her. She's blonde, thin, drop dead gorgeous, popular (especially with boys) and has worn a bra because she had to since she was eleven! It was only because Em, who is the nicest person I know, took pity on her when she joined our infant school that she became the third member of our gang.

The fourth and final member is Dave. We 'adopted' him when he started at our school a few years ago. He was pretty reserved then. Not surprisingly I suppose – after all, it's not every day that three beautiful girls take a boy under their wings! We have definitely brought out the best in him! My gran adores him. I've suggested she starts up his official fan club!

Gran lives in the country. She's more of a friend than a gran and we write to each other all the time. I can ask her whatever I like and she will always give me a straight answer, unlike my mum. Gran's quite eccentric really and has an excellent collection of bizarre stories to tell about herself and her family. For example, last summer she told me that she wore a wig! I was genuinely stunned, though my mum couldn't believe I'd never noticed!

I find it hard to believe Mum was the woman

who gave birth to me sometimes. She hardly knows me at all and since my little sister came on the scene, she has had very little time for me. Actually, I think I frighten her. I don't think she feels old enough to have a teenage daughter!

This book contains extracts from my diary and letters from last year. It's a collection of teenage trauma and, looking back on them now at the mature age of fourteen and a half, I can see the funny side to my dilemmas. I hope you can sympathise with them, but also realise that, with hindsight, things are never as bad as they seem. After all, everyone has experienced, or will experience, something similar at some point in their life.

Jayne Schwartzkopf

Chapter 1

2nd September

Dear Diary,

This book was an early birthday present from Gran, which I have decided to turn into a journal to record events in my exciting life!

It's only five days to go before the beginning of a new school year and I am filled with utter dread. I've skulked and mooched around like a real teenager-in-waiting all week since Emily left. I know that Meg and Dave have been feeling the same, but they can't possibly feel as bad as I do. Not a day has gone by without Em and me seeing each other for as long as I can remember. (That is excluding the time when she had the measles and my mum wouldn't let me see her in case I infested the whole house!) I think I might write her a letter, or is my mood too depressive or melodramatic? (No more than usual I'm sure!)

I'm seriously considering taking drama as an option at school this year. AARGH!! I can't believe I mentioned the dreaded 's' word again! That is the last time I will even think about it for the next five days. I'll make the most of the rest of the summer hols. I will write to Em and then drag Meg and Dave out for a milkshake! I really do hope that things will be the same now that Em's gone. I can't help worrying that everything will all start to fall apart.

2nd September

Dear Emily,
   This feels really weird, having to write to you instead of just knocking at your door. You've become another penpal, like Gran! It's just a good job that I love writing so much. You can guarantee that between us all, the ones you have left behind, you will be bombarded by letters. We're all missing you loads already. Meg keeps comparing how we are feeling to a death. She's so dramatic!
   Must go. I'm about to marmalize Vicky for pestering me as I'm trying to write. Let me know how everything is going. Don't forget, it's only twelve days to go until my thirteenth birthday! (As if you could forget!)
   Miss you.
      Love, Jay x

3rd September

My dearest Jane, sorry Jayne,
   I thought I would write because I was thinking about how full of woe you would be now that Emily has left. Just remember, change is something you have to accept, no matter how hard it may be.Your future is with Megan and David and all your other

friends at school – I can only remember Hester, Nick, Jacqui and Mary. I'm sure you are wallowing in self pity, feeling that you have been abandoned, dreading the thought of everything you have ever known, all your security, coming to an end. Live for the now. Don't harp on the past. Go out and get yourself a life! The sooner you do, the better.

   Love always,
      Gran x

4th September

Dear Diary,

   I knew when Gran told me that she was getting a satellite TV that it was a bad sign. She is obviously addicted to soap operas. Phrases such as 'Get a life' don't come naturally to someone who is over sixty years old and living in suburbia! I know she is trying to cheer me up in her own special way. The truth is, I am desperately lacking a life right now. How can I start to get one with all this up against me?

   1. I'm fat, ugly, spotty and slightly short sighted.

   2. I'm almost thirteen and have no obvious signs of approaching puberty other than loads of spots and some really weird hairs sprouting in even weirder places!

   3. My best friend has abandoned me and left me with Megan - God's gift to mankind - and Dave who would be more interested in what I was

me
↓

(a fat
spotty
balloon

saying if I had a disc-drive.

    4. I live with a constant pain – my sister Vicky.

    5. I am a stranger to my own parents.

    6. School starts on Monday.

    I am just filled with doom and gloom. I can picture myself now, on stage as Lady Macbeth or some equally tragic historical figure.

7th September

Dear Diary

    What a day! I woke up thinking I should take Gran's advice and that today would be the first day of the rest of my life. I don't think it will be easy if the days follow the pattern they started today. One good thing though: my hormones are not lying dormant as I had feared. They are really starting to party now because this is the biggest attack of teenage blues I have ever known.

    I'll start at the beginning. I dragged myself out of bed and put on my crisp new uniform. I called for Meg and we went round to Dave's house so we could all walk to school together. He never answered the door, but pulled back the curtain to show that he has a severe case of the chicken pox. I'm praying that I might have been infected with them, so I can have a few more weeks off school. Then again, he did look pretty awful.

    We got to school and met our new form teacher, Ms Regan the Vegan as she has been nicknamed already. She's a bit of a hippy, but can't be all bad because she is starting up a drama group. She gave us our intensely busy new timetable and I can tell that this is going to be a bad year.

That was just the start of it because my first lunchtime was spent waiting for Megan to come out of the loo. Just as I was about to send in a search party to find her she appeared, looking a bit weirder than usual. Then she told me that she had started her periods. Right there and then! I think I was more flustered than her. Luckily she has been carrying an emergency sanitary towel around for years now, in anticipation and preparation for her moment of glory – the most important signal of womanhood.

Unfortunately, this was the only one she possessed, so on our way home she made me stand in front of the personal hygiene counter in the chemist helping her choose the best sanitary towels to buy. She's eight months younger than me and she has started first. And she wears a bra. I've got to tell Em – she'll die of jealousy!

7th September

Dear Em,

Megan has started her periods. I'm sure she will have been on the phone to you already to let you know. I think she's trying to put a brave face on it all though because she did look rather pale and uncomfortable. She made me spend the whole afternoon reading the small print on the back of the mattress packets. Talk about rubbing salt in the wound!

How was your first day in the new school? Hope it wasn't too bad. Who am I trying to kid? I bet you've got hundreds of new friends fussing over you already.

Dave had a nice restful day at home. He's gone and caught chicken pox. He did look pretty rough this morning. Megan was very sympathetic, which I found quite unnerving because she isn't one of the most compassionate people we know, is she?

Let me know how everything is going and how you are settling in.

Love, Jay x

9th September

Dear Diary,

I'm up to my eyes in homework already. The teachers are starting as they mean to go on. One good thing – the drama group auditions are next week. The biggest surprise of the day was when Meg said she wasn't too interested in dramatics – she has enough of her own. I thought she might change her mind when Dave said through his living room window that he was keen. She wouldn't want to miss out on something.

I'm glad she didn't change her mind. She's becoming a real pain going on about her periods all the time. She keeps discussing them with Hester and Mary and when I look interested, she says that I wouldn't understand. I think she enjoys leaving me out of things.

I finally got a reply from Em:

Dear Jay,

Thanks for the letters. I'm missing you all tons too. School's not too bad, and I've managed to make a few friends, particularly with someone called Gaby. She lives just round the corner too. She's taking me horse riding shortly, so I'll have to sign off. Promise I'll write more soon.

Love, Em x

Now, that has to be one of the biggest anti-climaxes and shortest letters I have ever received. I pressed it onto Dave's window for him to read. He said it was nice that she was making new friends so quickly. Meg was as paranoid as I was, going on about Em obviously having forgotten us already, giving us only one letter to share between all three of us (especially after Meg has written and phoned her a few times) and that her mate Gaby (renamed Scabby now) sounded too good to be true. Dave didn't think Scabby would be a substitute for us and told us to stop worrying. He's such a sobering influence.

Surely Em must have more news to tell us? She's moved away from everything she has ever known and is making a brand new life, for goodness sake. She's just forgotten about us and is out to get herself this new life as quickly and painlessly as possible. And I can't believe she never even mentioned Meg's periods.

Megan was going to tell Dave all about her

14

periods. I thought it best to remind her that there was a plate of glass separating them and the whole neighbourhood would hear the conversation. Why did she think that he would want to know something that personal anyway? Admittedly, we do treat him like one of the girls, and he has sisters both older and younger than us, so he's not your typically ignorant thirteen-year-old boy, but I think he may have been ever so slightly embarrassed if she had told him. I wonder what sort of reaction she wanted from him. The mind boggles!

Oh, I prefer tampons myself. Megan, don't you?

10th September

Dear Gran,

Sorry I have taken so long to reply, but I've been so busy trying to get myself a life, as you advised!

Actually, if the truth be known, I've been overwhelmed by vast quantities of school work. There's a chance I could try and join a drama group. Dave is interested too.

Oh, and Meg started her periods. She is so pleased with herself. It reminded me that Mum has still not brought up the subject of 'the birds and bees' with me yet. I'm practically thirteen years old! It's a good job I've got you, Meg, Em and biology lessons, but it's not the same. I think I just intimidate her more and more as I grow older. What do you think?

Better go and do some more homework!

Love, Jayne x

15

P.S. Got a feeble attempt at a letter from Em. She's forgotten us already.

12th September

My dearest Jane, sorry Jayne,

You really do suffer from terrible paranoia and a fear of rejection. Do I sound like a 'shrink'? I remember my psychiatrist telling me that I could give him a run for his money! Emily won't have forgotten you at all, she'll just be all wrapped up in the move still. It's a big thing for her too. Try to put yourself in her shoes. She's got no choice but to try hard to settle in. Her parents aren't likely to come back just because she is unhappy and I don't think she's the type of person who would wallow in her own self pity. She knows that it was an excellent opportunity for her mum's career. But that doesn't mean she's going to wipe her past out just like that. You all mean a lot to her. You will all need to make the effort to keep the friendship alive, that's all. No one is saying it will be easy, but it can be done.

No, they just not

Me in E shoes

She's probably miserable but won't want you worrying. Try to be a bit more sympathetic. Imagine how she feels.

As for your analysis of your mother, I think you may have hit the nail on the head. I believe that your puberty frightens

16

the living daylights out of her. I remember
when she was your age, I found it difficult
to accept my baby was growing up. It's
quite a traumatic time for parents too,
you know. Adulthood brings a lot of
responsibilities which you will have to
face up to on your own. Your mum and dad
are trying to hold on to your childhood for
as long as possible to protect you from
everything.

   Glad to hear you have taken my advice and
are pursuing a more exciting life. Do let
me know how your quest is progressing.

   Love as always, Gran x

13th September

Dear Diary,

   My head is still reeling. First, I wonder when
Gran had to see a psychiatrist – and more to the
point, why? I always thought she was a bit loopy,
but I just put that down to her eccentricity. Wow! I
hope lunacy doesn't run in the family! Second, all
that advice about Em has made me feel terrible. I
have been so selfish. I don't think I've considered
just how overwhelmed she must be feeling right
now. Then third, all that psychoanalysis about
Mum and Dad. Phew! Gran can be so heavy,
man!

   Well, this will be my last entry in my diary as a
child, for tomorrow I will be a teenager. Wonder
if I am going to feel more mature or anything?

I'm getting all excited already. I won't be able to sleep.

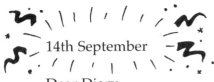

14th September

Dear Diary,

WHOOOOH!! Thirteen at last. I can't believe it has finally arrived. Mum keeps saying I'm wishing my life away.

I've had a lovely day so far. First of all, I woke up to breakfast in bed, lovingly prepared by my darling sister who has obviously had a personality transplant for the day. She even managed a less hostile than usual grunt. Then I got a card from Em. That really cheered me up and reassured me. She'd sent a parcel too, some stationery and a really posh pen so 'we have no excuses for not keeping in touch'. Ahh! She also apologised for the shortness of the last letter. She mentioned how jealous she was of Meg's periods and told me that even though she had heard the story in depth, both in verbal and written form, from the woman herself, she wanted my graphic account of it too. Then, Mum and Dad gave me a cheque instead of prezzies and have promised not to interfere with my decision on how to spend it. That is such a breakthrough. Sounds like they might actually treat me more like a grown-up now. I wonder how much Gran had to do with that?

Meg and Dave called round. It was Dave's first day out of isolation and he was raring to go. They had put their hard earned (in Dave's case at least)

pocket money together and bought me a CD voucher and a big birthday balloon. We went for a pizza and now we're off to the pictures. Gran has just rung. That is some indication of an event of major proportions because it's a ten mile drive to the nearest phone box. She ordered me to have a brilliant day, and I must admit that so far I have. I think that I'm going to enjoy being thirteen and I am determined to get a life. My teenager-in-waiting blues are over for good.

Chapter 2

15th September

Dear Diary,

I woke up this morning and definitely felt different. Maybe maturity can happen over night! I hope that it doesn't mean periods are on their way though. I've decided that the longer I go without them, the better. Poor Meg is still having the same one. That's over a week now! Apart from everything else, it's costing her a fortune! At least she's okay financially, what with an upwardly-mobile mother and stepfather throwing as much money at her as her heart desires, but I can see me having to get a part time job just to pay for mattresses!

School is taking over my life. Homework is being given to us like it's going out of fashion. It's lucky that I'm too fat and ugly to have a boyfriend because if I did he would finish with me for spending every waking minute reading and writing essays. I'm going to have no social life whatsoever for the foreseeable future.

However, Ms Regan the Vegan knows of my interest in drama. She said she thought I had thespian tendencies (and I took that as a compliment!). I have been practising my vocal techniques and Dave and I have been going over our scene from *Grease* without the singing because it's not our strong point. Let's hope the play isn't going to be a musical, or we don't stand a chance!

19th September

Dear Gran,

I've been totally dreadful to both you and Em for neglecting to thank either of you for my birthday presents. I know I said thanks when you gave it to me in the summer holidays (which feel like a lifetime ago), but I should have said it again. You will be pleased to hear that I do use the book regularly to record my deepest and darkest secrets. And, more importantly, I think of you every time I open it.

Lots of love,
Jayne x

Dear Diary,

I can't believe that a week has passed and I haven't thought of Em. Maybe I am coming to terms with the fact that she has gone. As Meg keeps reminding us, it feels like a death for us all. She, who has finally finished her period, may know what she is talking about after all. I know there are typical stages people go through when they are in mourning – denial, guilt, acceptance, grief. Perhaps we are entering the third stage now.

I do feel dreadful though because it means that I am getting used to her not being here and I never expected that day to come, especially not so soon. She'd hate me if she knew how I was feeling – after all I hate myself. Then again, Em is nothing like me. She is so forgiving and nice. She probably hasn't even noticed that I've not written back. Oh no! That would mean that she has forgotten all about me too!

20th September

Dear Jane,

You were a born worrier. Of course I am not mortally offended that you never wrote back immediately. In fact, it means that you have been too busy to think about letter writing, which must be a good sign. I'm positive that Emily will see it that way too. You are far too young to be so stressed out all the time. You should be footloose and fancy free. Just try to become more laid back!

Love as always,

Gran x

Dear Diary,

I happened to mention to Meg about my little bout of amnesia regarding the lateness of my thank you letters when she told me not to worry because Em had written to her and mentioned that she knew I was busy and expected a reply from me any day now.

Now, whenever I get a letter from Em, I show it

to the others immediately, but when the shoe is on the other foot, they don't bother. When I went on the rampage to Dave to moan, he looked all sheepish and told me that he had got one too. Apparently it had completely slipped his mind to show me. How, pray, did they forget to tell me something like that? Don't I count as someone who is interested in the welfare of my best friend? To be honest, I wouldn't have put it past Meg to withhold information about Em – after all, she has always been jealous of our friendship. She tries to convince herself and me that she is really Em's best friend. Maybe she is? But I really do feel betrayed by Dave.

Dave looking sheepish!

23rd September

Dear Jay,

I knew you would get round to writing eventually, not that I have been anxiously waiting for it or anything. Don't worry, there wasn't even the merest hint of sarcasm in that statement, so don't get all paranoid on me! I'm glad you liked your present though. Meg and Dave have told me how pleased you were with it and how much you were missing me. Aah! Nice to know I've not been forgotten already. The same goes here of course. I can't believe I wasn't there to share your most important birthday yet. Parents can be so cruel. I still haven't forgiven them for moving. Having said that, things could be worse here. Gaby is really helping me widen my social circle so now there's me, her, Donna and Gab's brother Patrick, so it's a tiny bit like the old days. Don't worry though, they are no substitute for you lot. How could they compete with the best friends in the world? Mum and Dad have said that you are all welcome to stay any time.

I'm trusting you to fill me in on all the gory details I am missing out on, Jayne! The more letters the better!

Lots of love,

Em x

Dear Diary,

I'm not surprised Em isn't finding it hard to fit in at her new school. Practically everyone in our year has asked me how she is doing and said that they miss her. I'm glad she misses us – I'm worried that she won't miss us for much longer though. I know it's silly, but she's so popular. I wonder what she sees in me sometimes. I'm so self-centred, but as my mum keeps saying, most actresses are, so I've already got one vital qualification in my favour!

25th September

Dear Diary,

Tomorrow is the big audition. I don't think I have ever been so nervous before in my whole life. My stomach is doing somersaults just thinking about it now, and the idea of us having half the school watching us at the same time will be horrendous. Still, at least there is one consolation. The man of my dreams, Jonathan Minter, may well be there if the rumours are true. PHWORR! He has to be one of the most gorgeous men I have ever set eyes on. According to Dave, he's really nice too. Imagine if he is there and I make a fool of myself on the stage. I'd die of embarrassment.

Still, there are more things to worry about. I went round to Dave's house to go over our lines one last time, and to my surprise, Megan called round. She obviously wasn't expecting to see me there, and looked rather uncomfortable when she saw me. I'm not surprised she looked uncomfortable – the clothes she had on were outrageously glamorous! She had a pair of those trendy hip trousers and a tight, figure-hugging top. She wasn't dressed to sit in someone's house all night, but that is exactly what she did.

It turned out to be quite beneficial because we had a taster of what it's like performing for an audience. But her actions were highly suspicious. She's really got me wondering what her ulterior motives were.

I can just see I'm not going to get a wink of sleep tonight – my head is reeling and my stomach is turning. I just know I'm going to freeze when I get up there. Please God, make it go all right!

26th September

Dear Diary,

I was so preoccupied with worry this morning that when my mum told me to break a leg I had to stop and think why the woman who gave birth to me would want me to endure such an injury! Whatever, it worked. We were excellent. By far the best there. In fact, I felt rather embarrassed for some of them. Poor Ms Regan sat there and looked so impressed with Paula Malone's rendition of *Somewhere Over The Rainbow* and Tracey Jones's *Summer Holiday* that she has really gone up in my estimation and must be a true professional in her art. The first few seconds on that stage I froze, but when Dave just went for it, I followed. It just felt so right to be up there. I have never been so pleased with myself. I'm still high on it. It was the biggest achievement of my life so far, if you exclude being my cousin's bridesmaid when I was six.

Dear Em,

Dave and I did it! We are officially in the school drama club. I wish you had been there for moral support. I have decided I am definitely in my element when I am the centre of attention. Now I know how Meg feels on a daily basis. She was quite impressed with us. Some of the acts were so bad that we looked like Oscar nominees! Jonathan Minter was there. He did this brilliant version of West Side Story, *and looked so good in his leather jacket!*

He got in too. Let's face it, Ms Regan had to choose him to ensure good ticket sales when we eventually do a play. He'd pull a crowd wherever he went! Oh, imagine if I had to act with him. Or even have a passionate stage kiss. What a thought!

Remember Mitzy Macmanus (how could you forget a name like that?). Well, she was pretty good too. I think we were too quick to judge her, just because we were so jealous of her dazzling beauty. She came over and told me and Dave how impressed she was with us. I thought that was really nice (either that or she fancies Dave – ha, ha) but Meg thought it condescending. She must be jealous of her talent or something.

Only three weeks to go until half-term. I won't be able to come down and see you then, unfortunately. Neither my nor my parents' budget will stretch to the train fare, but I'm desperately saving up. Maybe Christmas? I know that sounds such a long way away, but look how fast the last few weeks have gone.

For Hallowe'en, we're having our annual party. This year it's a fancy dress being organised by the sixth formers. I'm praying Jonathan goes. At least there will be something to look at when the conversation dries up or I'm left alone as Meg and Dave are pursued by rampant teenagers. I'm already sorting out my vampire costume (original, eh?). Dave is going as Frankenstein and – get this – Meg is going as Marilyn Monroe for some bizarre reason. (And I was under the impression that Hallowe'en is supposed to be scary!) Well, it's not that bizarre – she wants to look great while the rest *of us look even worse than usual.*

Wow, this is a really long letter! Hope all's okay.

Love, Jay x

4th October

Jayne, have you seen the noticeboard? Ms Regan wants the drama group to put forward suggestions for the school play. Can I call round after the match to have a joint thinking session?

Dave

Jay, can I tag along? I'm bored. Meg

I had this note pinned to my locker. Megan never ceases to amaze me. How can she be bored? This is the girl who can very easily spend an entire evening pampering herself with beauty products, and does it so often that she has been known to turn down many an invitation in favour of it. I'm starting to wonder what exactly is going through her mind. She's acting all innocent whenever I look at her inquisitively.

Meg the angel →

4th October

Dear Gran,

Hope you don't mind me asking your advice. If someone you knew was trying really hard to make sure she doesn't miss out on anything, even if this means being involved with something she has no

*interest in, dresses up to slob out in someone's
house, has started paying someone a lot of attention
and has even been laughing at his typically feeble
attempts at jokes, would I be right in thinking that
these are indicators of this someone fancying
someone else?*

*Good grief! Writing it down has only confirmed
my worst fears. It's perfectly obvious isn't it? If you
haven't put two and two together, I'm talking about
Meg and Dave! Urgh! It feels so incestuous even
suggesting it to you. He's like our brother! She has
loads of admirers. She could have her pick of any
number of boys!*

*Changing the subject rapidly, I hope Mum told
you the good news about my new theatrical
hobby. I am so pleased with myself. All we have to
do now is think of a good play to do. Any
suggestions?*

*I'm on my way to Dave's now. I suppose I had
better make a bit of an effort, and brush my hair
because Megan Romano, the glamour queen, is
coming along for the ride and will probably be
dressed to kill, looking ready once again for a night
out on the town. I don't know why she's bothering
when I always look like a tramp and Dave will
probably still be in his football kit. URGH!! She's
out to impress him isn't she? What a thought! Hope
you are well.*

*Lots of love,
Jayne x*

29

6th October

Dear Jane,

My dear, are you really so naive? Of
course Megan likes David and from the sound
of things, she's very keen on him indeed.
Have you even thought of the possibility
that they may already be an item? I don't
know why this disturbs you so much. I know
they are both like family to you, but are
they like family to each other? Not
everybody is as sentimental and romantic as
you are. You always see things in black and
white, but there are a lot of grey areas in
life. What I do know is this. You are all
reaching puberty at a great rate. I hate to
remind you, but Megan is getting there
slightly ahead of either you or Emily.
Therefore, her interest in boys is too. If
it is any consolation to you, I do think
that David is not quite on the same
wavelength as her. Girls do mature faster
than boys and he's probably more interested
in his computer and the football league
results. Having said that, Megan is very
pretty and I'm sure if she puts her mind to
something she usually gets it. If she pays
him enough attention, one day he will notice
her. Whether or not he does anything about
this entirely depends on him.

Changing the subject only slightly, I've
got the perfect play for you to do. *Romeo
and Juliet.* Now, don't let the idea of

Shakespeare put you off instantly. It is a beautiful and classic love story. You know I'm just a romantic old fool.

Any sign of you getting yourself a boyfriend yet? Don't tell your Mum that I said that. She's grateful you're not interested in the opposite sex. She thinks you are far too young. However, I wasn't far off your age when I met your grandad. He never noticed me until I was at least fifteen though. I think he used to have his eye on my sister Kathleen, until she married your great-uncle Joseph.

Well, better go. I'm missing the start of my favourite American soap opera.

Love,

Gran x

8th October

Dear Diary,

I put Gran's suggestion forward for the play. Dave put down *Reservoir Dogs*, another classic love story! For some reason, I don't think Ms Regan will take that one seriously.

I've been traumatised, wondering whether I should just come straight out and ask Dave if Meg has made a move on him. I think I know him after all these years. He'd probably be terrified by the very idea of it. Then again, maybe his testosterone level would receive such a boost that even if she hadn't made a move on him, I'd have planted the seeds of desire in his mind for her, thus doing her a favour! On second thoughts, maybe I should just keep schtum and wait it out. I'd really hate them to get together. Three's a crowd and all that, so who would I be able to go round with? And Dave's more my friend than hers. I'm not getting possessive or jealous – it's not as if I want him myself, but I don't want them to get closer to each other than to me!

And, another thing. Fancy Gran asking me about my marital status. As if I need reminding that I am young, free and single. Surely she must know that if there were any developments there I would tell her. Maybe she's hinting that I should start doing something about it now. After all, I know she's keen to have great-grandchildren! (I'd consider that if they were fathered by Jonathan Minter, but pigs might fly!)

18th October

Dear Diary,

The last day of the first half of term is here at last! HOORAY!

I have neglected writing my daily events up for a whole week now. Maybe I'm getting a life at long last. Drama club is going brilliantly, but I know that there is going to be a long, hard slog until we get even close to being ready for the play. Ms Regan decided to go for my idea and she's given us lines to go over in half-term for casting when we go back. I can see us now – me on the balcony and Jonathan underneath. And to think, Mum has no idea that I am having lustful thoughts for a boy who is practically a man! One thing is for sure, I am becoming totally besotted with him. I find myself daydreaming about him and admit that I have been practising my signature as Jayne Minter, or Jayne Schwartzkopf Minter, Mrs J. Minter and numerous other variations when I am bored.

Megan thinks I'm going mad. She said I'm becoming obsessed with him, as though she's never been like this. I've not mentioned anything to either her or Dave about the little situation, but the more I watch them, the more I think Gran was right when she said that Dave probably hadn't even noticed.

I do feel sorry for her now though. She's got her second period *already*! This one appeared totally unexpectedly. I told her that very few women settle into the typical twenty-eight day cycle straight away. She is in agony this time round. I'm so glad I don't have to worry about all that yet.

Chapter 3

20th October

Dear Diary,

Party, party, party! Half-term is here at long last! Dave and I are making really good progress learning our lines and I've told Mum that I needn't see any careers officers because I have found my true vocation in life! She was mortified! The more we practise, the more I can see myself in the role of Juliet. I'm not being big-headed, just quietly confident! Everything's mind over matter and if you want something enough, you can get it! What I really want is Jonathan. I am fantasising about him regularly. I am completely and utterly in lust with him (just like at least three quarters of the female population of our school).

I have decided to wait for the right moment to ask Meg about her and Dave, to avoid the possibility of offending her just in case I am wrong after all. You really would think that she would have told me herself by now (if it's true) if I were any kind of friend.

23rd October

Dear Jay,

I know that you owe me a letter, but let's not get petty. I've just had some juicy news I thought you might appreciate.

Megan has told me about the Marilyn Monroe outfit, which apparently has more to it than you may imagine. I find it quite refreshing to see that she hasn't changed and is still keen to spend her stepdad's money. She also went into graphic detail about her periods. From the sound of things, the longer we go without one, the better. They sound awful. Gaby started when she was eleven! She's a real expert now and has mastered the art of the tampon! ➡

Sorry! I'm waffling on here as usual. I'll get to the nitty gritty. Meg mentioned Dave. She said that she had been to a few of his matches to see whether or not he was the real expert he would like us to believe. At first, I was reading between the lines and thought that she was giving an excuse to watch Jonathan Minter in his shorts along with the rest of his fan club. But, on further investigation, I came up with another conclusion. They must be seeing each other. Not her and Jonathan, but her and Dave! Have you noticed anything to back up my theory? You must tell me immediately Jay! It's not like her to be so cagey about a boy, you know how much she usually revels in telling us all the gory and, more often than not, unnecessary details, so I reckon she must really

the art of
the tampon!

fancy him! Crikey! What a thought! Write back
as soon as is humanly possible.

   Love, Em x

23rd October

Dear Diary,

   My worst fears have been confirmed. For Emily
to come to exactly the same conclusions only
makes me realise how stupid I have been denying
it. I must ask Meg outright now. But imagine if we
were both wrong. Maybe she did go to the match
to see Jonathan, maybe she's trying to get to know
him better through Dave. If I did imply our
suspicions to her, there is a chance it would totally
alienate her because she hates the idea of anyone
attacking her reputation. No, I can't risk upsetting
her.

28th October

Dear Gran,

   *I'm really going to enjoy this half-term holiday.
The first seven weeks back at school are always the
worst! I'm doing well learning my lines and Dave's
not doing too badly either. I think it would be a
mistake of monumental proportions if we don't get
the leads! Eurgh – I just realised that that would
mean I would have to kiss him!*

   *Em has confirmed my suspicions about him and
Meg. Apparently, she's been secretly sneaking off to*

*watch his matches. Having said that, she's hardly
left the house at all this week as she's spent most of
it in bed with a hot water bottle pressed firmly to
her belly to alleviate period pain. Not really the
advertisement for womanhood she had hoped to be!
She looked terrible when I called round. I asked
Dave if he wanted to come and visit her with me,
but he declined. He said he didn't have time and
he'll go later. Mmm...I wonder. The suspense is
killing me, but I'm going to wait it out. On the one
hand, I'm practically dying to know, and on the
other, I'm dreading finding out.*

*Well, I'm off to get ready for this Hallowe'en
party. I've been practising my make-up all week. I
tried it out on Vicky and it must be pretty scary
because I made her cry!*

Love,

Jayne x

29th October

Dear Em,

*You missed a brilliant party. You were right about
Megan. She dragged herself off her death bed to be
there, the sign of a true professional party goer! I'd
expected the traditional vision of Marilyn in the
white dress, but she came as the long-dead movie
star, and the mouldy dress wasn't half as glamorous
as I had expected. She looked really good, and
original too!*

*I noticed at one point that she was alone. I was
with Chris so I didn't give it a second thought, but*

37

later on she was still there. I watched as the occasional male flickered towards her like moths to a flame, but her spark just wasn't there. I thought maybe she was ill, but when I went over and she said 'Jay', I knew what was coming next.

We have been right all along. But when my fears were confirmed, all I could do was stand there in shock, mouth open, saying 'Dave? Our Dave?' (So much for the forewarned, forearmed theory!) Apparently, according to Hester and Jacqui, who were right down the other end of the hall, I squealed the words at such a decibel level that I could be heard over the music! Half of the partygoers, including the man himself, turned round. He thought there was something wrong and looked very concerned. Thankfully, I managed to deter him from coming over with a smile and a wave!

Poor Meg, though. When I finally picked my jaw up off the floor and got my vocal chords going again, I asked if Dave knew how she felt. She said that the ignoramus had no idea. I can believe that. I tried apologising for my far from casual reaction and we spent the rest of the night discussing it. She asked me if I would mind if she went out with him. How ridiculous. Of course I mind, but I told her it was none of my business and said that if she was asking my opinion, it would be to keep the 'just good friends' scenario and told her that confessing her lust for him would be the wrong move to make.

Is that really so terrible? Surely that's the sensible thing to do, but I feel so guilty. She went on to tell me that she has only realised lately how considerate, sensitive, caring and – get this – attractive he was.

Then she told me that she'd not said anything to me because, deep down, she knew what I would say, and that my advice was probably right, BUT...she didn't think her feelings for him could change back to the way they used to be!

I wonder if she will heed my advice or not? Maybe if you tell her the same thing then she will. Write back soon to let me know.

Love, Jay x

30th October

Dear Jane, sorry Jayne,

Just a little note to wish you luck in your pursuit of the role of Juliet.

Have there been any further developments on the Megan and David front? Change is a fact of life, like it or not. Nothing stays the same forever – things would be pretty boring if they did. I think the best thing you can do is stay out of it and leave it up to them. Otherwise, you might end up losing one or both of their friendships over your interfering.

Love as always,

Gran x

Dear Diary,

Gran has made me think about the situation even more. Maybe Meg and Dave would be right for each other. Perhaps I am standing in the way of a beautiful relationship. I'm going to make a conscious effort to be nicer and a better friend to them both, whatever the outcome. They both mean too much to me to risk throwing their friendship away. Thus speaketh the new, mature, thirteen-year-old (but still no sign of a period) Jayne Schwartzkopf.

2nd November

Dear Diary,

The die has been cast. I was so nervous, but Meg said she couldn't tell. I'd learned my lines so well that I just went on auto pilot! I was pleased with how well I did – pity Ms Regan the Vegan wasn't. She gave Juliet to Mitzy Macmanus and God's gift to womankind, Jonathan, got Romeo.

What a missed opportunity. I'm going to spend years wondering 'What if?' now. I can't believe I let that one pass me by. If only I had tried harder. Still, what chance did I stand of getting a role that is played traditionally by drop dead gorgeous women? Still, I suppose I should be grateful that I got a part at all. And I do get the chance to stand on stage at the same time as Jonathan. We even do a few scenes together. I'm the nurse and Dave's Mercutio, Romeo's friend, which is quite a big part too. He was brilliant. I felt really strange watching him perform – must have been pride or something. I could almost hear Meg's heart beating wildly for him as she watched. Oh, I'm so cynical. In hindsight, I don't think the way

THUMP! THUMP!

she was watching him was lustful. I've got a
terrible feeling that there's more to it than that. I
think we could be talking the four letter word
here. LOVE!

3rd November

Dear Jay,
   Thanks for the letter. I'm so sorry I wasn't at
the party. It sounded brilliant. We never did
anything half as exciting here. We just went to
Gaby's house to watch a few spooky films. I
told you I was right about Meg! I get the
impression from Dave's letters that he hasn't got
a clue that he's the object of her desires, bless
him!
   Are you all going to the firework display at
Sefton Park on the 5th? I wish I was back there.
I haven't missed doing that for a single year
until now. We're all going to Donna's for a mini
display, but things won't be the same. There's
going to be loads of people there for me to get
to know, but sometimes I just don't feel like
making the effort. I just want to be myself with
people who know me, like you lot! I have this
idea that they are only trying to be friendly
because they feel sorry for me. Do you think
you could all come down over Christmas? I wish
you would, just to show you off to everyone and
say, 'Look, I'm not sad really, I do have friends
but they just don't live by me any more!'
   Maybe I could come and see you instead? It

Em's real
friends

41

would be more like the old times if I did. Then I could catch up with everyone from school at the same time. Would your mum mind if I stayed there? I'm sure I could stay at Meg's, but you know how finicky her mum is – I always feel like I should take my shoes off when I walk on the carpets, or feel guilty if I crumple a cushion on the settee! Write soon, old chum. Missing you all loads.

Love, Em x

Dear Diary,

Poor Em. She sounded so miserable and lonely. I can't imagine how bad it must be for her being there. I'm glad at least she's got Scabby Gaby. And how can she think that people are only being friendly to her out of sympathy? She's the most popular, friendly and likeable person that I know. Everyone who comes into contact with her loves her. I've never known her be so unsure of herself before. I think she'd better come down over Christmas so we can all cheer her up. Better ask Mum nicely if she can stay. I'll make a start on the dishes and keep in her good books.

5th November

Dear Em,

Just a very quick note to tell you that my mum said yes for Christmas. It's not too far away, so cheer up. You are a wonderful person and people talk to you because they want to. You are lovely! That's why we are all depressed back here without you! I'll have to go if we are to get a good speck for the fireworks. I'll be thinking about you all night.

Love, Jay x

Dear Diary,

Just got home. The fireworks themselves were even better than I remember, but things were different. For the first time, we were all together and it dawned on us that Em was missing and things would never be the same again. We got really melancholic and went for a milkshake and talked for hours about the old days! We were getting more full of doom and gloom, when Dave reminded us that she'll be back in a month and that we just have to get used to her not being around. He's right. He usually is. I suppose I can see what Meg sees in him after all.

Chapter 4

8th November

Dear Em,

Went back to school today. I still keep expecting
to see you around. Rehearsals for the play start this
week. You will not believe what happened to me
today. Me, Dave and Meg (who was there because
she always has to be in on everything) were
standing in the corridor discussing when we are
going to get any time to do anything else other than
act. ('Real professionals have to suffer for their art'
and 'No pain, no gain' are Ms Regan's favourite
sayings. I'm sure we are going to be sick of hearing
them by the time Easter's here. Eek! That sounds
such a long way off. We haven't even had Christmas
yet!)

Anyway, getting back to the point, there we were
talking when Jonathan Minter walked past. The
palpitations in my stomach started immediately.
Then he saw us and came over. I tried so hard to
keep my cool and act casual, but when he smiled my
knees just buckled! He started talking to Dave and I
just stood there mesmerized by his sparkling eyes. I
was in daze when I realised that he was talking to
me. I was so flustered I couldn't understand what he
was saying, so Meg had to do most of the talking for
me. He said 'Hello Nursey'. His voice is so deep. I

*tell you, he could call me anything and I wouldn't
mind. Then he started talking to Meg, as one would
expect, and asked her why she wasn't in the play
too, to which she replied, 'Oh, I'm not that
talented or outgoing'. Then she spent ages with
him discussing her inadequacies and creeping up
to him by telling him what a talent we had all got,
and how she wished she could excel at something
too.*

*When he said 'bye', I felt like I'd had the wind
knocked out of me, and Dave made me feel
ridiculous. He went on about how embarrassing it
was to see me drooling all over him and how
pathetic girls can be over some boys. Can you
believe that? I was, and still am, so upset. Why
would he say something so cruel? I haven't spoken
to him since and have no intention to either until he
apologises. Meg told me not to take it to heart so
much, but I have.*

*Anyway, changing the subject to something
lighter. The Christmas disco is on the 21st. Will you
be able to come down for that? Let me know soon so
I can get your ticket.*

Love,

  Jay x

Dear Diary,

I don't think I'll ever be able to sleep again. I
can't believe I made such a fool of myself in front
of the man of my dreams. Dave was right. I was
embarrassing. The words 'Hello, Nursey. What's
your real name then?' keep spinning over in my

head and then the most cringe-some words that I ever said in my whole life follow like some kind of nightmare. 'Jayne, with a "y"'. Oh, my cheeks are burning just writing it down.

No wonder he turned his attentions to Meg, standing there as a sophisticated contrast to my idiocy. I hate her more than ever. She just took it all in her stride and kept a full conversation going with him with no trouble or effort at all. She was gazing up at him all gooey-eyed, when it should have been me! One minute she's professing undying love for Dave and the next she's flirting with any male in sight.

Oh! Jayne with a 'y'. I want to curl up in a ball and die. Why is nothing ever easy for me? If my name was Meg, then that would be a different story.

12th November

Dear Jane,

How are you, my dear? Working hard I hope. Not long to go until you come down for Christmas. I just hope that you don't have to turn down too many social occasions because you'll be here! Let me know how you are doing in the rehearsals.

Lots of love,
    Gran x

13th November

Dear Gran,

Sorry to have to tell you, but my social life is chronic at the moment. There's vast amounts of homework to slog through every night, loads of rehearsals and to top it all, I'm not speaking to Dave and am finding it really hard going with Megan too. Dave said some really hurtful things to me, which gave my self-confidence a huge blow and I still haven't forgiven him. I made a total fool of myself in front of the man I want to marry and Megan is so perfect it makes me sick.

As you can imagine, I'm counting the days before we come to see you and am dying to get away from all this. There's only that and the school disco, which Em's coming back for, that is keeping me sane. Can't wait to see you.

Love,

Jayne x

16th November

Dear Diary,

Just come back from a marathon shopping spree with Meg. The amount of money she spends on clothes could feed a family of four for a week. It's impossible to find any suitable disco outfit when you are shoved in a room that is lit with the most unflattering illuminations you have ever seen, with a million other girls who are all in the super model league. I always manage to be the one who has every spare ounce of puppy fat hanging out when the tall, thin, gorgeous girls come in and strip down to their teeny tiny underwear right next to me!

And Megan doesn't help. She could put on a binbag and look excellent. The only wobbly bits she has are exactly where they should be. She spent the majority of the day stuffing her face with chocolate and fizzy drinks, and does her skin ever break out in spots the size of volcanoes? I think not. She just has everything going for her and I've got nothing. Why is life so unfair? Why can't I be the one who is pretty, blonde, popular and eating vast quantities of junk food and never turn into a blob? I'll probably look like a shiny, white balloon in the shirt I ended up buying. ➡

Actually, thinking about it, Meg was very keen for me to get it. She's probably having a good laugh about it now. She's always telling me how jealous she is of my figure and no matter how convincing she may sound, I can't help thinking she's having me on. Mum and Gran are always telling me skinny girls look unhealthy to make me feel better, but how come they always get the clothes they want in a size that fits, and above all, suits them? How come *they* are always surrounded by a flock of male admirers, are always gorgeous and have a personality to kill for? I hate everything!

16th November

Dear Jane,

I am truly shocked by the news that David said something to offend you. Are you sure you didn't twist what he said and take it the wrong way?

Don't forget, he's probably feeling confused too. Puberty can be rough on boys as well, especially if their best friends are girls. He's most likely noticed that you are changing and he's probably a tad 'freaked out' by it all. It would be terrible if you did let this come between you though. This is practically the twenty-first century, and girls should take it upon themselves to sort out their lives, not wait for the men to do it for them. Seize the day - life's too short to waste.

As for this boy at school, I hate to tell you, my dear, but the chances are he never even thought twice about this horrendously-embarrassing incident you spoke of. Self-confidence is something which comes with age and life experience. On the other hand you have got destructive self-consciousness. You get embarrassed, worry, get more embarrassed and so on. It's a vicious circle that you are going to have to break out of, otherwise your life is going to be miserable. You are always saying how comfortable Meg and Em are with the opposite sex. Take some tips from them - the first

step forward though is to start liking
yourself, and regardless of how you are
thinking now, you do have a lot going for
you.
    Love as always,
        Gran x

23rd November

Dear Jayne,
  All I can say are two words – JONATHAN
MINTER! Good grief! I bet your feet still haven't
touched the ground after your little encounter. I
don't know how you managed to speak to him
at all. I'd have been so stunned that he had
lowered himself to speak to us plebs in the first
place. I wouldn't worry about Meg having an
in-depth conversation with him either. You know
how she revels in situations like that. She could
have a conversation with anyone, and often
does. Don't take it to heart so much. She said
that it was really cute how you reacted to him,
going all red. If she was any kind of normal
person, she'd have gone puce too. If it was me,
I'd have given him sunburn with the heat that
would have radiated from my face, so don't
worry! She just has this natural coolness when it
comes to boys. I've yet to see her flustered by
them at all. I'm convinced that you have either
'got it' or not. Obviously, we haven't. But at
least we are friends with someone who does, so
that's bound to come in handy. Gaby's like that

too. Makes you sick doesn't it?

The disco is a definite yes, by the way. I break up from school earlier than you so would it be okay if I came down the night before? I know you have to go to school the next day, but I'm planning a little surprise for the old gang. Let me know if it's okay and I'll book the train tickets.

Are you speaking to Dave yet? I've never known you two to fall out. You and Meg, yes, but Dave? Maybe it's your hormones! He hasn't written for a while. He is okay isn't he? Send my love to everyone, including him. That means you are going to have to speak to him and I'm going to put you on a big guilt trip now by saying ▶▶ otherwise things won't be the same for my first visit back. I want things to be exactly the same as before! See you very soon. Can't wait.

Love,

Em x

25th November

Dear Diary,

Between the two of them, Gran and Em have disagreed on a few things, such as sexual charisma being something you are or you are not born with. But the fact that they both made me realise I'd be silly to lose Dave's friendship over all this has made me have a good think about the whole situation. There's only one problem – he did hurt my feelings and I still don't think it should be me who makes the first move. I never insulted him, did I? But Em's guilt trip has worked. Things wouldn't be the same for her, so for her sake, I think I'll be a real woman and go and see him.

As for the subject of charisma, I prefer to agree with Gran. After all, she's had sixty odd years' experience. But, having said that, the likes of Meg do seem to have more than their fair share of it naturally, because she just oozes it in certain situations. Maybe I could ask her for some practical hints. Oh no! Bad idea. It'd be like me admitting defeat and she'd feel like a real, mature woman then. It'd boost her ego no end. She'd feel so superior then. But who am I trying to kid? She is superior. I can't waste my life waiting for fate to get round to me, I've got to get out there and grab it myself.

Chapter 5

26th November

Dear Em,

Absolutely brilliant news that you will be down for the disco. You'll be pleased to hear that Dave and I are speaking, thanks to you! Even though I am still the innocent party, I called round and asked him if I could walk to school with him this morning. He looked really shocked to see me there, but agreed. We never said a word until we were practically on Meg's door step, when he said, 'Jayne, I'm sorry. I was totally out of order,' to which I replied, 'Yes you were,' then I gave him a hug. Perfect timing for Meg – she opened the door on us and her face just dropped! It was a picture. She said 'Oh, speaking again are we?' and has been a bit weird with me all day. She's probably jealous. After all, she's had Dave all to herself for a while now! Even Dave, who as you know is not one of the quickest people in the ways of the woman, noticed her reaction. He said, ' You'd think she didn't want us to get back together, judging by that reaction.' Maybe he's right!

Well, see you on the 21st.
Love,
Jay x

31st November

Dear Gran,

I have been busy building bridges between Dave and myself, you'll be pleased to hear. I swallowed my pride, and approached him and he apologised straight away. He must have had a really bad attack of conscience over the past few days. I'm really glad things are back to normal again, more or less. Megan's being a bit cool with me. I'm convinced she's jealous that we have made up. She must have enjoyed having Dave all to herself!

Talking of Meg, I'm going to analyse her techniques with the opposite sex like you suggested. I'm not going to ask her for hints outright, she'd love that too much. It would be like me admitting how bad I am where boys are concerned, and she would just revel in the fact I had to ask her for advice. Once again, my pride rears its ugly head. See you soon.

Love, Jayne x

5th December

Dear Diary,

The rehearsals are killing me. I'm wondering if I've bitten off more than I can chew. Having said that, Dave manages to fit in football too, as does Jonathan, and he's got his big exams this year too! He smiled at me *three times* this week, so he must have forgotten or not noticed my stupidity the other week. Either that or he was laughing at me when he remembered! We had to rehearse Scene Four. For the first time I had to act with him. I thought we were pretty good together. If only I'd got Juliet! Anyway, he must have thought so too, because he put his arm round me and said, 'Well done, Jayne'. JONATHAN MINTER TOUCHED ME!! HE REMEMBERED MY NAME AND THOUGHT I WAS GOOD! I am so in love with him. I wonder if he knows? Maybe he thinks the same about me! I've never seen him have physical contact like that with any of the other girls, not even Mitzy!

10th December

Dear Jayne,

Just thought I'd let you know that the train tickets are booked and I'll be getting to the station at about 9 o'clock on the 20th. Will you be able to meet me? Can't wait to see you all.

Love,
Em x

11th December

Dear Em,

Of course we will be there to welcome you back. Only nine days to go, and counting!

Love, Jay x

P.S. By the way, Jonathan Minter hugged me!!

55

22nd December

Dear Diary,

What a weekend! I'll start at the beginning.

We met Em at the station as arranged. We were all so nervous waiting for her, it was weird. When she finally arrived everything just felt as if she'd never been away. Within seconds, all my worries about things not being the same had gone. It was excellent.

We spent the whole of Thursday night talking and in the end Mum had to come in and chase Meg and Dave back home and remind us that we had school in the morning. We carried on talking for ages after they had gone, so getting up in the morning was a bit of a chore. I think that when I'm older, facing work after a hard night at a club is going to be a problem for me!

I'd forgotten she had a little surprise for us, and when I asked in the morning what she planned to do with herself while I was at school, she replied, 'Come with you!' She produced her old school uniform from her bag and said that she'd just have to talk my mum into letting her try to sneak back into school. I was amazed when Mum agreed and said she couldn't see any harm in it! Dave and Meg thought it was a brilliant prank too, and when everyone at school saw her, it took them a few minutes to register! She spent a good fifteen minutes in the biology lesson before Miss Skarratt batted an eyelid and that was because Hester and Nick couldn't control themselves any longer and burst out laughing. In the end, Miss noticed and for a moment I panicked and expected a class detention, but she saw the funny side too, and we spent the rest of the lesson catching up with Em's news. Miss Skarratt was really good about it all but said that there was only one problem, that we had done no work all lesson so would have to get extra holiday work. Surprisingly, I didn't hear anyone complain. It was the perfect way to celebrate the end of school.

The night of the disco finally arrived. Em and I spent hours getting ready and I felt pretty snazzy. I told her that I was going to be a big vamp and make a play for Jonathan. When we called for Meg, the thought instantly went out of my head. She looked brilliant in this figure-hugging teeny tiny dress, curly hair and loads of make-up on! (I wish my mum was like hers. I could just about manage to leave the house with a smidgin of mascara and a hint of lipstick on!) How could I possibly stand a chance of winning Jonathan while there are hundreds of girls in her league after him too? We all trooped round to get Dave. He gave us all a wolf whistle and said he'd be the envy of all the lads, turning up with three gorgeous women on his arm! I told him that he could talk – he looked brilliant too. Meg's face was a picture when she saw Dave. I can see what Dave meant now when he said that my reaction to Jonathan was embarrassing. How he could have failed to notice Meg's tongue practically tripping her up is beyond me!

The disco was great! Everyone was there and Em was in her element, flitting between them all and catching up with them. This didn't bother me

– after all that's what she does best. But when Meg disappeared and Dave went to the loo, I was left all alone. That turned out to be the turning point of the whole night because Jonathan came over to me. I mustered up all my confidence and took a deep breath. It was my second chance and I wasn't going to make a mess of it like last time. I managed to keep the chit chat going quite well and amazed myself at how cool I remained when Meg came back. Within seconds, she had taken all his attention and was once again showing me how the experts do it.

I could stand it no longer, and before my anger erupted, I excused myself and walked away. I bumped into Dave and he knew something had happened. He spent about ten minutes trying to calm me down. I wanted to kill her! She *knows* how much I like him. I just can't have anything to myself without her wanting it too. Dave was able to talk me into trying again and not letting her get the upper hand, so I was about to rejoin the conversation when I caught the two of them SNOGGING!

HOW COULD SHE DO THAT TO ME? AND I'D ONLY BEEN GONE FOR A MATTER OF SECONDS TOO! Talk about fast worker! If Dave hadn't been there, I'd have committed a murder. It makes my blood boil even now. I ran to find Em because I couldn't bear being in the same room as Meg for a moment longer. Dave went to tell the harlot (who had by then come up for air) to make her own way home with Mary and Hester. We walked home in silence. I felt like my heart had been torn out. What a brilliant Christmas this is going to be now.

Em went home today. Dave and 'her' turned up to say goodbye. 'She' was acting so normally that I was doubly offended. It was as though she hadn't given me a second thought. I could barely look at her, let alone speak to her. But I didn't have to speak because she never gave anyone else a chance to. We were forced to listen to all the gory details about how he told her he liked her the first time he had spoken to her in the corridor, and that he'd been dying to ask her out ever since. How can she have forgotten our little conversation about her love for Dave so readily? She's so fickle! I wonder how long this 'love' is going to last?

She finally finished putting me through hell and eventually noticed how uncomfortable I was and said, 'Oh Jay. Are you all right?' I was so proud of my self control and I just said, 'You know how I feel about him,' and left it at that. She looked sheepish and Em broke the awkward silence by reminding us she had a train to catch.

We got to the station, exchanged Christmas presents and gave Em one final hug. It felt awful to see her go – just like the last time, but worse.

We were all so depressed that no one said a word on the way home. That suited me fine, otherwise I'd have ended up strangling Meg. I finally broke the silence by saying to Dave that I'd see him after Christmas and gave him a hug. I ignored Meg completely. How can I call her a friend after this? I'm glad I'm going to Gran's so I can sort my head out.

Chapter 6

24th December

Dear Diary,

Here I am again at Gran's. The journey here was fun-filled. Trying to keep myself amused with only Vicky for company in the back of a car is not one of the best ways I can think of to spend four hours. She really is hard going. Sometimes I'm convinced that *she* has teenage attitude, not me. Then we had the little problem of the car breaking down in the middle of nowhere and Mum and Dad having a row over whose fault it was, before poor Dad had to walk off into the wilderness in search of a 'phone.

We finally arrived a few hours ago, with varying degrees of hypothermia! Gran managed to warm us up instantly with big hugs, an open fire and lots of tea and home made biscuits! I love coming here. We are all spoiled rotten. Having said that, I've still got so many things on my mind. Gran and I are going to have a good chat about everything later on. She's the only one who seems to understand what I'm going through. I wish Mum could be more understanding sometimes. It's almost as though she was never a teenager herself. Either that or it was all so traumatic for her that she's blanked it out of her memory. She told me earlier to cheer up and not spoil Vicky's Christmas! Is she the only one who counts? What about me for a change? If I feel like wallowing in self pity, then I'm certainly not going to pull myself out of it just for the sake of little Vick! I think I'll go and be melodramatic for a while.

I have returned. I had a really good chat with Gran as we did the washing-up. She made me realise that I should be more tolerant to Vicky. I also opened my heart to her about Jonathan, and told her that I don't think I could ever find him attractive again after he's kissed Meg and responded so quickly to her flirting. They're two of a kind and obviously meant for each other, but I'm still hurt by her doing it to me.

25th December - Ho, ho, ho, Merry Christmas!

Dear Diary,

I've been awake since approximately five o'clock this morning thanks to my never ending wriggling and questioning by Vicky. If I had heard, 'Has he been yet?' one more time, I'd have killed her. Thankfully, she dozed a little bit but woke up at the crack of dawn and was like a child possessed as she hurtled herself down the stairs and seconds later made a frenzied attack on a pile of presents that had been innocently waiting under the Christmas tree! I have to admit that it was brilliant to watch. Now I know what Mum and Gran meant when they said that Christmas is for children. She got some brilliant presents, but I bet she won't let me near them. I got loads of things too. I am really lucky I suppose to have such a nice time at Christmas.

26th December

Dear Em,

I've had a brilliant time, did you? Were all the family round at your new house? Is it big enough to fit them all in? I wish my mum had a few sisters or brothers, or Dad was a bit closer to his so we could all get together like you do. I've told Gran all about Jonathan. She said that he sounds like 'a bit of a hunk'. (More vocabulary from all those soap operas!) She said that boys like him are usually trouble and I'm best out of it anyway. She told me that I'd do better if I went for someone like Dave! I'm convinced that if it was possible, she'd arrange our wedding. I told her that that may be true, but love is blind, and I'm blind as a bat where Jonathan is concerned and only have eyes for him. She finally agreed that, no matter how much sensible advice people give, it's human nature to listen, but try things out for yourself before you believe them.

We had a great time when you came down. I'm saving up for my ticket to yours. Is Meg going to visit you shortly? I heard her talking to you about it, but I think she should wait until we can all afford it and go together. After all, you know it won't be the same without me or Dave there too! (Okay, I admit I'd be jealous if she went without me!)

I've been thinking about her and Jonathan and have

decided that she's welcome to him. Okay, I liked him,
but there's plenty more fish in the sea, and they're
bound to have better taste in women than him!

Have a great holiday, what's left of it anyway!
Write soon.

Love, Jay x

28th December

Dear Diary,

It's time to go home already. Time flies when
you're having fun and as always, it's been brilliant
here. Gran and I have just had our ritual walk
along the beach. I love that place. It's just
wonderful there. I can't wait for the next school
holidays to come back. Oh no, mentioned the
dreaded 's' word again. There's just over a week
to go before we go back and there's still loads of
homework to do before them! GROAN! I think I
lied to Em about Meg. I just can't forgive her, even
if it is the season of goodwill to all men (and
women). I still can't believe she did that to me!

30th December

Dear Jay,

Thanks for your letter. Glad you had a good
break at your gran's. I heard from Meg. She
had a lousy time as usual. She went to see her
dad but felt really bad when she had to leave
him alone again and go back home. It must be

really difficult for her. Have you forgiven her yet? I think she needs her friends around her now, Jay, and like it or not, you are one of them. I know she's taken Jonathan from you, but like you said, it's not that important anyway. You should go and see her and make it up with her. I don't think she'll be coming down to see me. Apparently, she and 'Jon' are seeing quite a bit of each other and she took him to see her mum and step dad on Boxing day. Mum and Dad wouldn't allow me out of the house if I had a sixteen-year-old boy friend, let alone condone it like hers do!

Going anywhere for New Year? We are piling round to Gaby's house. I'll be thinking of you lot (as the song goes 'Should old acquaintance be forgot...' Don't know the rest of the words, but you get the gist!) Have a think about what I said about Meg.

Love, Em x

Dear Diary,

I'm back home and was met with this letter that really pricked my conscience. I had a long think about everything and finally thought that she was right, so went round to Meg's. She seemed quite pleased to see me and I apologised for being so juvenile and possessive over someone I had absolutely no hold over whatsoever. She said sorry too because she knew how much I liked him, but was attracted to him herself after he'd flattered her so much and she knew that what I had said about her and Dave was right – that they should never get together because it would spoil their friendship. Then she said that if I was in her shoes, would I say no to the most handsome boy in the school? It was then I could see her point of view. He is irresistible to all womankind and I felt that I had played quite a big part in bringing them together because I had put her off the idea of making a move on Dave.

Thinking about it now, I'd prefer her to have Jonathan than Dave. It won't cause half as many problems, although she can't have loved Dave as much as she thought, otherwise what I said wouldn't have made the slightest bit of difference. Then she told me that Jonathan is having a New Year's Eve party and he wants me and Dave there because he thinks we are really nice! I can't believe it! I've got an invitation to the party of the year! Em is going to be so jealous!

31st December

Dear Gran,

I'm just writing to say that I'm missing you already and can't wait to come again soon. Mum and Dad have agreed to let me go to a New Year's Eve party tonight, without a chaperone. Dave and I were invited by Meg (yes, I've sort of forgiven her) to Jonathan's party. Have a happy New Year. I've got to go and pamper myself in preparation for tonight.

Love, Jayne x

Chapter 7

1st January   HAPPY NEW YEAR!

Dear Diary,

I can't believe that a year can be over so quickly. Mum said that that's one of the first signs of old age creeping on.

Today, the whole Schwartzkopf family have a variety of ailments. Mum and Dad are nursing their annual over-indulgence headaches, Vicky is slightly less hyper than usual following her first ever experience of a New Year (she is normally tucked away in bed) and I am, for a change, and the perfect way to start a new year, depressed! But, I suppose that I should be grateful for at least I brought in this year with a bang, which must be better than the usual boring ones that slip in silently while sitting watching the telly.

Before the party, Dave and I called round to Megan's house to pick her up. She, as always, looked like she would have felt more at home parading across a catwalk. Meg said that she wasn't quite ready, so we waited for ages while she preened herself to perfection, every brush of the hair and wave of the mascara wand making me feel more inadequate and insignificant!

Finally, we arrived at Jonathan's very swish

home twenty or so fashionable minutes late! Meg and he are two of a kind, just judging by the vast wealth they both share. There were literally hundreds of people there, all spilling out over the lawn and driveway. I recognised loads of kids from school and there were several adults there too, which would have put Mum and Dad's mind at ease if they had known. Within seconds of us arriving, Meg had spotted 'Jon' and was off like a shot.

Even though I still had Dave for company, I felt rather uncomfortable. It was obvious that we were the youngest there and it felt like everyone was laughing at us trying to play grown-ups. Dave said that I was being even more paranoid than usual and that we should have been making the most of our first real New Year's Eve party. I decided that was the best attitude to have so we started to rave!

The house was like a palace inside. It also resembled a brewery with vast amounts of alcohol everywhere, and to my amazement, we were offered some. I did feel rather tempted to try one of these marvellous cocktails and I got the impression from the people in the room that if I didn't, I would have taken the brunt of their jokes for the rest of the night.

I was told that the only way to drink this concoction properly was to 'knock it back'. Then I got nervous and wanted to change my mind, and I looked to Dave for some assistance. He was just glaring at me as if to say, 'You asked for it' and I knew that he was going to leave it up to me to sort the peer pressure out. I must admit that I was just about to give in, when I smelled coconut. I explained that I am allergic to it and heaved a sigh of relief as the glass was swiftly removed from my hand and replaced by another. In the nick of time, there was a lot of wild screaming coming from another room, which thankfully distracted everyone and they finally left me alone.

Dave said that he had never seen me squirm so much before and I told him that a real friend would have helped me out. He said that he wanted to see how easy it was to pressurise me into something and said that I should have just said that I never wanted the drink in the first place and take the risk of being laughed at, which would have been better than going home drunk! He was right, but I was tempted to try it. The most alcohol that has ever passed my lips has been in the form of some liqueur chocolates that we had last Christmas, and they only made my throat burn and my eyes water. I was just about to ask him if he had been tempted when I remembered the bad time his mum had had with the drink not long after baby Luke was born. Thankfully, because her problem was sorted out quite quickly, I'd forgotten all about it, but I came very close to reminding Dave of it. That really sobered me up (terrible choice of words there!).

Later, Dave and I had a good dance and chatted to some of the more approachable and less pretentious of the fifth formers (which must have been a maximum of four or five!) and we hardly clapped eyes on Meg or 'Jon' all night. I finally

spotted them in the middle of the crowd, dancing
to a slow song. She was draped all over him. It
made me feel ill. It was like a form of torture
watching them and it made me realise that, no
matter how hard I tried to convince myself and
everyone else otherwise, it was going to be
difficult for me to accept their relationship.

A wave of depression suddenly hit me and I
was dreading the big twelve o'clock snogging
thing because I was bound to be sitting in the
corner like a wall flower. I decided the best thing
to do would be to skulk away until all the hype
was over with, so I sat outside in the garden for a
while and Dave followed me. He asked me why I
was hiding but I could hardly tell him to leave me
alone, that I hated myself for being fat and ugly,
that I despised Megan for having Jonathan and
that I hated the whole world, could I? So, I told
him that I'd got hot to which he replied, 'Oh, and I
thought it was because you'd seen Meg all over
Jonathan.' As always, he made me laugh. It was
exactly at that moment we heard the music stop
and the countdown for the New Year start.
We didn't bother to move inside and when all the
party poppers went off, we just looked at each
other, said 'Happy New Year' and...well...I felt
pretty uncomfortable, awkward even, and he
looked all sheepish, so we met in the middle. I
was aiming for his cheek and I think he was
aiming for mine, but I got so embarrassed that I
just ended up brushing my face against his and I
stood up quickly to go back in.

The way he looked at me made me feel so

strange and I got this weird sensation in my stomach. I can't explain what exactly, but it was like nothing I've felt before.

We walked back to the house in silence, and the first thing we saw was Meg and Jonathan sitting on the stairs. Meg had her head in her hands and 'Jon' looked the worse for wear himself with a huge bottle of something, obviously not lemonade, in his hand. We ran over and Dave grabbed hold of Meg. She was semi-conscious having been plied with drink by Mr Minter himself. (She regularly has wine at home, so she must have consumed quite a bit to be in the state she was in.) Dave helped her up the stairs to the bathroom and I was ready to follow, when Jonathan grabbed my arm. He said that he had wanted to speak to me all night. I told him that I would rather go and see to my friend who was rather unwell because of him. I am so proud of how cool I was, especially as I was so angry too. How dare he do that to her! He knows how old she is!

Then it suddenly dawned on me that Jonathan Minter, the sex god himself was holding my hand! For a split second I was too stunned to move. I thought that he had finally noticed me and was paying me the attention I'd been craving for months and I thought that at last everything was going to follow my great plan of things! Amazingly, I wasn't far off the mark! It took him all his time to speak (as his speech was slurred), but he told me that he thought I was really attractive and tried to snog me!! My wildest dreams were coming true, but unbelievably I found myself pushing him away. The smell of alcohol on his breath, the way he had to hold the wall to stand up straight and the fact that he obviously couldn't focus on me put me off. In fact, I was repulsed by him, especially as then I remembered that he was Meg's boyfriend. I rejected him, after having done nothing but dream about it happening for months!

Unfortunately, from what I can work out now, both Dave and Meg arrived at the top of the stairs a few seconds too early to see that, and had only witnessed the bit before when he was doing his impression of a letch. We must have looked guilty thinking about it and Meg jumped to a few conclusions. Dave said that she had been sick in the loo and had sobered up almost instantly. Then she had been met with the sight of the two of us in a compromising position, went quietly back into the bathroom and started screaming. All that I knew was that I could hear her screaming, so ran up the stairs to be confronted by her doing a realistic impression of the wild woman of Borneo and Dave telling me to make myself scarce while he calmed her down. I decided that taking into account that the alternative was Meg tearing my hair out, his suggestion was a good one.

I ran past Jonathan who by then had another form of female attention and I went back into the garden. There were a few people out there, and I tried to be as inconspicuous as possible, but someone noticed me – Mitzy. She came over and tried to play the good Samaritan.

At first I was wary, but she seemed genuinely

concerned to see me upset and before I knew it, I'd told her everything! I said that Megan was going to hate me for something I never even did (but had wanted to if circumstances had been different). That was when Dave and the woman herself emerged. I wasn't sure if I should have run for cover, but decided to sit it out, otherwise I might have looked even more guilty.

She screamed at me for a few seconds and then stopped abruptly, probably because I wasn't arguing. I just stood there and took it all. When she had calmed down Mitzy took her to one side and started talking to her. When I looked at Dave, I could sense the resentment in his eyes. I told him that nothing had happened and that they had jumped to the wrong conclusions. He must have found this difficult to accept as he knew how much I had (past tense) liked Jonathan and I was too tired to try to convince him further.

Mitzy went to ring us a taxi and afterwards called me over to talk to Megan. She was trying to be a good mediator but neither me nor Meg were in the mood for discussing it any more, so we sat in silence. I think she gave up trying to put things into perspective for us after a few minutes and went off to talk to Dave. They spent a while talking (probably about us) and I never even looked up until I heard the taxi arriving.

Chapter 8

2nd January

Dear Gran,

I am so depressed. Am I such a terrible person? I have managed to start off a brand New Year without my best friend Emily and now I've lost Dave and Meg too. They caught me in a compromising position with Jonathan, but never gave me the opportunity to explain and now I don't think I should tell them the truth if they are that quick to judge me. The fact is that I said no to his advances but they're never going to believe me. What am I going to do?

Love, Jayne x

4th January

Dear Jay,

Happy New Year! Let's get down to the nitty gritty. What has been going on back there? I heard from a distraught Meg about her finding you in a passionate embrace with her Jonathan! Is this true? I can't believe it? Was it worth all the aggravation then? Is he a good kisser? Are you seeing him officially now? Didn't you feel even the slightest bit guilty over Meg? I'd better tell you that I told Meg not to jump to conclusions until she had talked to you about it, but she said there was nothing you could say that would make her change her mind about what she saw. You have got to write back and tell me all the details straight away. I wish you had a 'phone in your room like Meg. She can talk so freely! Hurry and let me know all!

Love, Em x

4th January

Dear Jane,

Oh dear, my dear! What a mess you have got yourself into. First of all, well done on refusing the advances of a male. Secondly, we have the problem of convincing David and Megan of your actions. Why don't you write to them and explain if they won't listen? That way you wouldn't have to face them and you can say what you need to without any interruptions. I do think that it would be wise to set things straight, before Jonathan gets to them first and twists facts to suit him. If he is the rat that you say, then Megan needs her friends. Good luck and move fast.

Love as always,

Gran x

6th January

Dear Diary,

Two days before we go back to school and I am
still dithering over whether to act on Gran's advice
or not. I know she's right, but it's easier said than
done convincing them – besides, I shouldn't have
to. They should believe me anyway. Even Em has
chosen to believe that I would do it, as though I
have no scruples whatsoever. And, how can I
persuade them to see my point of view when I *was*
tempted. Would I have refused him if he had been
sober? I can't even be honest with myself over that
one. Maybe I would have snogged him if he hadn't
smelled like a brewery. I can't believe that I have
lost all my friends in a matter of months. I must be
a terrible person. This probably serves me right,
divine retribution and all that.

7th January

Dear Jayne,

I suppose you will be shocked to hear from me.
I thought that I should sort this out once and for
all. The fact that you have not made the
slightest effort to come and apologise or even
explain about the other night only makes me
think you have a guilty conscience. Jon told me
everything and you hardly made it a secret how
you feel about him. I know he's popular and I can
handle the other girls being all over him, but for
my best friend to do that to me seems

unbelievable. I can't understand why you made a move on him when he was obviously vulnerable and I was ill. It's just so low Jayne, but I thought I should let you know that your little plan didn't work and that we are still together.

Meg

Good grief! What can I say? Things just keep getting worse and worse.

8th January

Dear Gran,

Went back to school today. It was hell. I never got a chance to write to Meg and I'm glad I didn't because she got there first. It was so nasty, she obviously doesn't want to hear my version of events. Thankfully, Dave had second thoughts. It's his birthday today. He knocked for me this morning (probably to make sure I've got him a present) and he said that he has had time to think things over, and that whatever happened, it's got nothing to do with him. He said that both me and Meg were his friends and he wants to remain neutral. It took him all week to decide this though.

It took me a few minutes to forgive him, but I did because it was his birthday and I need at least one person to talk to or I'll go mad. I'm glad he came round. I've got a feeling this rift is going to last for a while. Hope you are well.

Love, Jayne x

To Dave.

10th January

Dear Em,

I am here to defend myself. I am so upset that you could even consider Megan's version of events as fact before I had been given the chance to explain. Both she and Dave jumped to the wrong conclusion and now you have too. You may be surprised to hear that, unlikely though it may seem, I said no to Jonathan's offer of a snog.

Has Meg told you that she sent me a lovely note? She heard his story and believed it, and I can't be bothered even trying to change her mind because she must have such a low opinion of me. She has spent every possible opportunity at school talking about me in a loud voice, swanning around with the man himself (who looks like the cat who got the cream).The self control I am showing is spectacular. I feel like lunging at him, not to snog him either, but to kill him! Still, if she prefers his company to mine, then that's her loss. He'll dump her soon and what's the betting she'll be round here as soon as he does?

Thankfully, after days of deliberating, Dave is remaining neutral. I hope you never forgot his birthday. He said he didn't want any fuss so we've done nothing to celebrate, which I feel bad about. He's the only friend I've got. Everyone's whispering about me behind my back and you know what a vicious tongue Meg has got on her. I dread to think what stories she's spreading. I wish you were back here. I rest my case, your honour!

Love, Jay x

JON'S EX GIRLFRIEND

14th January

Dear Jane,

Hang in there, my dear! Megan will come to her senses soon enough. At least you have still got David. I vividly remember falling out with my best friend over a dress. I spotted it first, but she bought it before I could get the money together. It did suit her, but she wore it once and accidentally tucked her knickers in it! I let her wander around like that for over fifteen minutes before I told her. She was so grateful, she apologised profusely!

I know it's not quite the same situation as you find yourself in, but I hope it's brought a smile to your face. Keep your chin up!

Love, Gran x

P.S. Would it really be such a bad idea if I suggested you going to see her to set the record straight, or would that mean too much pride swallowing?

20th January

Dear Diary,

I'm still thinking about Gran's recommendation, but I'm still in two minds over it. I saw Mitzy today as Dave and I were perusing the new rehearsal timetable. She was asking me how things were with Meg and said she'd noticed 'they' were still together and asked Dave what he thought. Mr Sensitive replied that he hates disagreements between friends and it is especially annoying when it happens because of girl/boy friends. He said the problem with us is that we are both as stubborn as each other. He's right. One of us is going to have to make a move or it will just drag on forever. I know she drives me mad most of the time, and she irritates me beyond words, but I miss her!

30th January

Dear Jay,
    Please forgive me for being such a terrible letter writer! I owe you an apology. I am amazed by your self control and just presumed that you would have given in to Jonathan's advances, like the rest of the female population. Sorry! Hope you can find it in your heart to forgive me. I should have known you better than that!
    Also, regardless of how you may feel towards Meg, and understandably so, I thought I should remind you that you did the right thing. I'm going to tell her your side, because I know you'll be dithering over what to do and I want to see this sorted out. She's got to know that he's lying to her and she should be wondering how many other girls *haven't* resisted his charms!
    It's almost half-term, and you had better be

talking by then, otherwise you will be so bored!
Maybe, after I tell her, you could go and see
her face to face. That way you will be showing
her your superior maturity. Have a think! Do you
really want him to get away with it?

Love, Em x

Chapter 9

13th February

Dear Diary,

I got all excited unnecessarily this morning, thinking I had a Valentine's card. I should be so lucky! Upon further investigation, I discovered I recognised the writing, and to my horror realised it was Megan's. I wasn't in the mood for another written assault, but my curiosity got the better of me. It said:

Dear Jayne, I'm sure that I am the person you least want to hear from right now, but I really need to speak to you. Please call over as soon as you can. Meg

I couldn't believe her audacity! As though I would just drop everything and go running after all she's said about me. I asked Mum what she thought and she said it sounded serious. Before I knew it, I was ringing her door bell.

She looked as uncomfortable as I felt when she let me in. As soon as we were in her room, she burst out crying. I didn't know whether I should comfort her or not, but decided I should. After all, anything could have happened. I was getting rather worried and my vivid imagination was going into overdrive thinking up a variety of horrendous scenarios, when she got her breath back and spoke. She said how sorry she was and she should have trusted me and before I had a chance to say anything, she told me that she and the 'lying toad' were finished.

My reflex action was that of relief because of the mental images I had conjured up and my second was relief that she had finally seen sense. I was heading for the angry mode when she said that she had ended it. I wondered whether I had heard her right and she must have sensed what I was thinking and said that he had told her that their relationship needed to be 'livened up and moved along a bit faster'. Me, the master of reading between the lines, thought the worst – that he had forced her into doing something she didn't want to and I was just about to climb on my moral soap box when she reassured me that she'd done nothing about his ultimatum other than tell him what he could do with it!

Apparently though, the super stud didn't take this too well and said that as far as he was concerned, he had ended it because she was immature and he wasn't bothered anyway because he could have his pick of the girls who had been waiting patiently for him. What a rat!

I sat there in disbelief over the whole situation. Megan had split up with Jonathan Minter! She is so strong and never lets anyone walk all over her, that's one of the things I most admire about her. She knows exactly what she wants, and sticks to her principles, even though I am sure she considered his suggestion. She said that she realised that she had probably found herself in a similar situation to that which he put me in at New Year and apologised for not giving me the chance to explain.

The worrying thing now is what Jonathan might do. Megan thinks he may spread some untruths about her. (I know the feeling well.) We thought that Dave would be the one to see about that. After all, he's in the changing rooms with him before matches and that must be one of the places boys choose to brag about girls!

Unfortunately, he wasn't in when we called round at his house. He'd gone to the park to take Luke for a walk. Meg went all gooey again and remarked on his sensitivity. Surely she can't be so fickle as to transfer her emotions back to him the day after the big split? Just when I think things are going my way again...!

14th February

Dear Em,

Well, another Valentine's day has come and gone. Did you get many cards? I had to fight my way through them myself.

I'm just going over to be tortured by Meg as she's probably got hundreds as usual. Yes, in case she's not had a chance to tell you, we are speaking again. I expect you know all about the pervy Jonathan's outrageous proposition he made to her. Who does he think he is? I'm going to make the most of Meg's

humbleness! There's nothing she won't do for me at
the moment if I asked her. There is only one little
problem back here in paradise. She's trying to pick it
up with Dave where she left off! Can you believe her?
Then again, at least that'll be taking her mind off
getting all depressed. Oh Em! How could you leave
me to console her on my own? You know how she
revels in her woefulness! I'll let you know how she is.

Love, Jay x

16th February

Dear Jane, sorry Jayne,

I hope it's okay for me to write to you
now and not be mistaken for a Valentine's
card like last year. How many did you get?
I wouldn't worry if there weren't too many
- you are still only thirteen after all.
You still have the best years to look
forward to. Has the situation with Megan
been resolved yet? I hope there have been a
few developments.

Love, Gran x

17th February

Dear Gran,
Thanks for your letter. Surprisingly, I didn't
receive a single card. I bet the postman loves me!
Still, I wasn't allowed to wallow in self pity for too
long because I spent most of the day desperately

light as
a feather

trying to avoid the significance of the day for the sake of Megan, who has finally seen the light and finished with Jonathan. She apologised, just like you said she would, after she saw his true colours.

She only got two cards herself this year, which was quite disappointing for the girl whose record is seven! There were no clues on either of them, but with the help of Dave, we have discovered the culprits to be friends of his — Derek and Nick. Apparently, between the two of them, they have started up their own Megan Romano Appreciation Society. They cheered her up somewhat. (If that was me, it would have made my life, not my day!)

Dave got two himself. Meg has admitted to sending one but the other is a bit of a mystery. It's signed 'M', but Meg said that she left hers blank. Seems she has a rival in love.

It was Dave's birthday a few weeks ago now, but it was while we were being juvenile and not talking to one another. Neither of us made a big fuss of him because we were too wrapped up in our own problems, so we threw a little party for him at Meg's house last night. It was really to say sorry and thank him for being friends to both of us and he was really touched by it. The usual crowd from school came and we had a brilliant time. I think that's all my news. Does it sound like I'm finally getting a life yet?

Love, Jayne x

P.S. To add to my inferiority complex, even Vick got a Valentine's card. As you can imagine, she has been unbearable to live with.

85

19th February

Dear Jay,

Thank goodness you have sorted yourselves out at long last. How do you think Meg's handling this whole Jonathan thing? She sounds quite together about it but you know how she bottles everything up when she's depressed.

Changing the subject somewhat, do you think you'll be able to come down over Easter or will you be going to your Gran's? I know that you have got the play to worry about before then, but I want to start arranging things back here if you are all coming. Let me know as soon as you can.

Love, Em x

1st March

Dear Diary,

It's been quite a while since I last had time to write. There are only three weeks until the play and we've been rehearsing to death. Dad has said that he'll video it for Gran because she can't be there. I wish she could be. Jonathan has been playing it very cool and according to Dave hasn't said anything out of line either. Sounds too good to be true if you ask me. He 's probably just watching his p's and q's while Dave's around.

I'd better go. It's Vick's birthday party and the house is overrun with little kids screaming and flicking jelly everywhere.

8th March

Dear Em,

Have I got news for you!

Today started off as a typical Sunday. The three of us had gone for a walk around the park with Meg's dog. We were on our way for our ritual milkshake when Dave said he had to go. We didn't think too much of this until we saw him walk off in the wrong direction for his house. Our curiosity got the better of us, and I'm ashamed to say we sneaked off after him to see where he was going. It wasn't really spying, honest! Meg, who was doing a very lifelike impression of Miss Marple made me stay with her because she was desperate to solve the mystery. We didn't have to wait long as he stopped at the bus stop. When the bus came a few minutes later, he was engulfed in a cloud of carbon monoxide and it felt like hours before it lifted. You are not going to believe what we saw when it did. There he was, walking hand in hand with Mitzy Macmanus!! We were totally stunned. Neither of us could believe what we were seeing! Has he mentioned anything to you about her? Let me know if you have any juicy gossip to fill in the gaps.

Love, Jay x

P.S. I'm sure Meg told you, but we'd love to come down over Easter, that is presuming Dave can bear to be torn away from his beloved! (I am still in shock!)

Dear Diary,

I am still in shock, but there's more to it than that. When I saw him with her, my heart almost stopped. I felt sick. How could he be seeing her without even mentioning it to us? We always tell him our secrets. He obviously doesn't trust us the way we do him. Poor Meg looked like she wanted to throw herself under the bus! It's all she needs right now. At least it's kept her mind off Jonathan. It's obvious why she's upset but what's worrying me is that *I'm* feeling upset too. In fact, I have never felt so jealous before. He *can't* have a girlfriend! Any girlfriend would probably be jealous of his friendship with us. Does this mean he's going to leave our cosy little circle? And even if it doesn't, will we want him in it any more – he can't be as close to us as we thought, or he'd have shared his secrets with us. That's what friends do.

Chapter 10

14th March

Dear Gran,

There's less than two weeks to go before the play. There have been a few minor setbacks, such as the main costume maker having broken an arm and Capulet (Nick, Meg's number one fan) tore a ligament in a football match, but besides that, everything is ready! Dave and I have planned to go over our lines AGAIN, but that was before the events of last night.

Megan had invited us both over to her house for dinner. As you know, Meg's 'dinners' can be very grand affairs and I was almost considering hiring a ball gown for the evening. It did turn out to be interesting, because she had invited a surprise guest too – Dave's new girlfriend, Mitzy Macmanus (Juliet in the play). We spied the two of them meeting up last week, but I've been trying hard not to let him know that I know, because if he'd wanted us to know, he'd have told us. Meg said that she had accidentally (I wonder?) put her foot in it and told him everything. I could kill her – we'd planned to act all surprised when (or if) he told us!

Anyway, Meg thought it'd be a good idea to invite her, and get all our questions answered by the

woman (and I do not use the word loosely!) herself.
She said that she had to invite her to show Dave
that we are prepared to make the effort to get to
know her better, for his sake. This would be a very
mature thing for Meg to do at the best of times,
but it's especially amazing as she is once again
besotted with Dave, so there's bound to be ulterior
motives to her little plan. I still have to find them
out though.

I must admit, Mitzy's presence made me feel
uncomfortable. We were all on our best behaviour
and tried very hard to make things as natural as
possible, but all I could think of was how she
seemed to be filling the gap left by Em. From then
on, everything she did annoyed me – and this is
someone who I like, or at least, used to like!

Meg eventually got Dave to spill the beans on the
origins of the big romance and, reading between the
lines, it sounded to me that she had basically put
him on the spot so he couldn't refuse! I'm not
surprised he didn't refuse – she's older than him,
really pretty and they have loads of things in
common. They even looked quite good together. But
I'm still not convinced they are meant for each
other.

Why am I finding it so hard to accept he's got a
girlfriend? Do you think it's because,
subconsciously, I'm worried about him doing a
vanishing act like Megan did, or because I'm
worried what Meg has got up her sleeve? I'm sure
Megan's not going to let him slip through her
fingers for a second time, and she's hardly likely to
let me convince her otherwise now!

Dave
spilling
the beans

Would it be okay if I came to visit in the Whit holidays, on my own for a change?
  Love, Jayne x

16th March

Dear Jane,

What a marvellous idea about you coming down alone. I'll have a word with your mum. I'm sure it won't be a problem though. You know I'm going to miss seeing you at Easter, but I know how much you miss Emily, and I was the one who told you if your friendship was so important you would have to work at it! I'm glad you are.

You asked for my advice on the latest little situation you find yourself in and I'll tell you, but I don't think you are going to like it!

To me, it sounds like the reason you are being hostile with this Mitzy is because you are jealous of her - not of her looks, or her talents, but the fact that she has landed David! You may have been right when you said that she is invading your space and your own cosy world, just like Jonathan did, but there could be more to it than that!

You are going to have to be very honest with yourself if you are to sort anything out. Decide whether or not I could be right, and we'll draw up a plan of action

```
when you come to see me.
    Love, Gran x


    P.S. Good luck with the play! I'll be
thinking about you.
```

20th March

Dear Diary,

Gran's advice has knocked me for six. She has suggested that maybe I like Dave so much I want him myself! I can't believe she has suggested such a thing – the whole idea of it makes me feel ill! Or maybe, as the saying goes 'The woman doth protest too much'. Maybe there is some truth in it! Perhaps she's right! Perhaps that's why I've suddenly begun to dislike Mitzy and maybe that was the reason I told Meg not to ask him out!! My head is reeling! I'm so confused. I've been embarrassed to look at him and I'm sure Mitzy is picking up on the bad vibes I'm giving her. How am I possibly going to be able to concentrate on the play now? It's only four days away!

Mum and Dad are taking us out for their anniversary, so I hope that takes my mind off it. I don't think I'll be able to face the food though. My stomach is in knots.

21st March

Dear Diary,

I feel burned out. How Dave has fitted in football practice as well as the play amazes me.

He's still with Mitzy, looking happier than ever and whenever I see them he's all over her. I've decided that whatever my feelings for him, and I've still not decided what they are exactly, I'm disregarding them and from now on will grit my teeth and make an effort with Mitzy. She's been trying so hard to be nice since I was horrible to her the other night at Meg's. If I just accept they are together and take myself out of the equation, it'll make all our lives easier.

He is still coming to Em's with me next week but there's been a change of plan for Meg. She mentioned her plans to her mum but was told she couldn't go. This was followed by a big argument and finally her mum had to tell her she had arranged an early thirteenth birthday surprise – a trip to Florida! It was no surprise which one she chose. I am *so* jealous. She's pretty, thin, wears a bra because she has to, has periods and has so much money it's sickening. Life is so unfair – some people just have it all.

Having said that, maybe, just maybe, this has happened for a reason. She was talking about Dave the other night and said that she was going to start work on him in earnest over the next few weeks. She said that she didn't think there was enough 'spark' between him and Mitzy, so it shouldn't be too hard, but she thought it best to wait for a week or so until the novelty of it all wears off for him! Maybe this is the opportunity for me to do something about my (possible) feelings for him before she gets her claws in. I'll have a while to sort my head out at Gran's soon, but maybe our trip to Em's might help me unravel my inner turmoil, because we're going to be alone on the train for hours!

24th March

Dear Gran,

What a night! I just had to write because there was no possible way I could sleep after the big performance, I'm so hyper. It all went really smoothly, even though I was a bag of nerves. The fact that when the floodlights are on you can't see any of the audience apart from the front row helps, but you just know that the room is bursting at the seams, and every eye is on you. I thought that I would seize up, but I'd learned my lines so well, they just flowed. I even played the true professional and gave it my best shot with Jonathan, who I have done a brilliant job of avoiding and ignoring for the past few weeks, and with Mitzy, who I have decided to bury the hatchet with. Ms Regan the drama teacher made a mistake casting Jonathan as the lead – Dave upstaged him in every scene. He was just brilliant. You can see for yourself on the video soon.

We got a huge standing ovation and Miss Pritchard, the head teacher, told us that she had never seen such a professional amateur performance in all her career, and that Ms Regan was an asset to our school.

Afterwards, we had a big get together, but the party is on the last night. Mum and Dad came and they said they were really proud of me, and I think they meant it, too! That was just the perfect end to one of the best nights of my whole life! I wish you could have been there too.

Jonathan came over to me. I wasn't sure if I should have given him the time of day, but he seemed harmless enough and Megan was too busy talking to Dave and Mitzy to notice. He seemed genuine when he told me that he thought I gave a good performance and then he apologised for upsetting Meg. I told him that I appreciated it, but I was sure she'd prefer to hear it from him herself. I saw him go over and her reaction wasn't as explosive as I was expecting. She kept the upper hand and later told me that he ate bucketfuls of humble pie and admitted to being a male chauvinist! From the twinkle in her eye when she was talking, I wouldn't put it past her to forgive and forget. She thinks he might have changed! Leopards don't change their spots do they – especially so quickly? I've since heard through the grapevine that he has finished with Phyllis, so he's obviously on the rebound looking for another replacement. He and Meg are very similar really – neither of them like being on their own for very long. I wish I had a choice in the matter!

Amidst all the excitement, I noticed Dave was on his own so I went over to tell him how brilliant he was. I gave him a hug but as I pulled away and *looked at him something really weird happened. For a split second, it looked like he was going to tell me something, but he changed his mind when Mitzy appeared on the scene. She seemed a bit cool with me, or maybe it was my imagination.*

I still haven't reached any conclusions about what's happening, but I know that things are changing between me and Dave, and he probably knows it too.

I had better try to get some sleep, still another two performances to go!

Love Jayne x

26th March

Dear Diary,

Last day of term again and the last ever performance of *Romeo and Juliet* is over. It was so sad, especially when Jonathan presented Ms Regan with her bouquet at the back stage party. It felt dreadful packing away our costumes, like the end of something special. We are going to try to twist Ms's arm to get her to do another play, maybe for Christmas. After all, what else are we going to do with all the free time we'll have on our hands now?

Jonathan and Meg are being very civilised with each other. He seems to have had a personality transplant and, if I'm not mistaken, there could be the possibility of a rekindled romance in the offing. I told her she'd be stupid to take him back, but she said I don't know him like she does. The thing is, I do know that she can be easily impressed and I think she'll be taken for another ride if she falls for the flannel a second time. This does prove my fickleness theory. One minute she is swearing undying love for Dave, then she forgets him at the drop of a hat, then she loves him again and then she forgets him for a second time. I can't work her out.

I left them to it – there seemed little point interfering. She's old enough make her own decisions. Nick came over to see if things were back on with them. He looked like a little wounded puppy as he limped away. He is so nice and is absolutely besotted with her. She could do a lot worse for herself, and I've a terrible feeling that she is just about to!

Dave left early – alone! He looked tired, but said that he'd be over early in the morning so we could make an early start to Em's. I'm so looking forward to having him all to myself on the train and have decided to see if I can get to the bottom of what is going on between us. I can't wait to see Em.

27th March

Dear Jane, sorry Jayne,

Congratulations! Your mum rang to tell me how fabulous you were in the play! I always said you had that star quality about you! Hope you have a fabulous time at Emily's.

Love, Gran x

27th March

Dear Gran,

 This is just so typical of my life. Nothing ever goes according to plan. Never again will I put my faith in fate or destiny. Instead of Dave calling for me this morning like he said he would, he rang to tell me he had flu! (He's always ill lately. I'm sure it's because he's vegetarian.) Megan (who will be at the airport now) got me wondering if he was making up excuses because it would mean him leaving Mitzy for a whole seven days! Surely he wouldn't let me or Em down like that, would he? The very fact that I am questioning his integrity only proves that I feel I don't know him any more! Is he changing, or just growing up, growing apart or getting himself a life that no longer includes us? Maybe we have served our purpose and he no longer needs us. Do I sound paranoid to you? (Oh no, sorry, you'd call it lovesickness!)

 I half expected Mum to tell me that I couldn't go on my own, but thankfully she never did, so here I am, alone on the train, feeling very grown-up but with the weight of the world on my shoulders!

 Have a wonderful Easter!
 Love, Jayne x

Chapter 11

7th April

Dear Gran,

I had a brilliant time at Emily's! Her new house is beautiful, her room is amazing and her whole family are just thriving on the changes. They all look so well!

I can understand them moving away more now I have seen their new life for myself. I had been so worried about meeting all her new friends and the possibility of feeling left out, jealous or inadequate, but they made me feel so welcome and I was fussed over by everyone! I feel so much better knowing her situation now and that she's got some good friends. I also feel reassured knowing that there is still place for us in her life too.

I met Gaby (formerly known as Scabby — my arch rival in Em's affections). Her brother, Patrick, was lovely too. In fact, he was gorgeous and even though I had gone there with my mind full of problems over Dave, I never gave him a second thought thanks to Pat's attention. To cut a long story short, I kissed him! My head is still somewhere in the clouds now. I am in love, Gran, and it feels brilliant! Write soon.

Love Jayne x

7th April

Dear Diary,

I just can't get Pat out of my head. I didn't want to come back home because of him (and Em, of course). I was having such a good time there. I'm depressed about being back and Mum thinks I'm becoming anorexic because I'm off my food, which is a first! Vicky thinks I'm going insane because every time she sees me, I've got a smile on my face. I know I'm acting strangely and I'm dying to tell the world I'm in love, but I know what their reactions would be – Vicky would laugh in my face, Dad would get embarrassed, then get mad and Mum would never let me go to Em's again. It's not worth even hinting to them.

I still can't believe I've had a snog. And, more importantly, it wasn't as disgusting as Meg had said it was. I'm sure she was put off the first time because she wasn't expecting Barry McKeown to thrash his tongue around so violently in her mouth. However, it wasn't enough to deter her from trying it again! Mine was just *perfect*, with a handsome, blond, blue-eyed fourteen-year-old hunk. It makes me go hot just remembering it!

We'd finished the barbecue and were watching a fantastic sunset. I am going to be eternally indebted to Gaby and Donna for going in to tidy up and to Em for getting more drinks, because they left us alone. That's when he told me that he was going to miss me and put his arm around me. Mmm. I can still smell him now! I froze, not so much with fear as with shock! Then he leaned over to kiss me. I thought I was going to die, and realised that it could have been a distinct possibility because I can't remember breathing! It wasn't a big, sloppy thing, but a nice, gentle kiss. It was so perfect that he's probably done it before. (Who am I trying to kid! Of course he has – he's a hunk!) I wonder if he knew it was my first one? Oh, my face is getting hot now remembering how we must have looked when Em came back. I never let her get a wink of sleep all night! She said that she was jealous, and that he was rated as another Jonathan Minter in her school. (And I used to think he was unique!)

We were laughing about how envious Megan would have been if she had been there. Imagine if she had. He'd have probably snogged her instead! Oh, he is gorgeous. I'm expecting him to ring any day now. I thought he might have done already, but I'm sure he doesn't want to look too eager and will play it cool. I can't wait to see him again. I wonder if Gran would be mortally offended if I went to see him in the Whit holidays instead of her? She is an old romantic after all, and it would mean that I was finally getting a life!

9th April

Dear Dave,
I thought I would write in case I ran the risk of catching any germs from you. I'm home and wanted to know if it was worth me knocking for you in the morning. Let me know tonight please.

I had a fabulous time at Emily's. She sends her love. Did you get a postcard from Megan? I think she must have sent it in the airport for it to have got here so quickly! Sounds like she's got some news for us. Hope you're feeling better.

Jay x

10th April

Dear Em,

How are you? Recovered from my visit yet? Please thank everyone again for me, especially your mum for making me feel so welcome.

I've not heard from Patrick yet. He is all right isn't he? You know how over-active my imagination can be. I'm missing him like mad, and have been thinking about nothing else since I got back. I wish he'd given me his phone number. Will you check that he hasn't lost mine? He said that his parents were really strict about girls, but he must be able to get to a phone. I'm considering coming down again. Would that be okay? Do you think Pat's changed his mind about me? Oh no. What if he's realised he's made a mistake. Please write and cheer me up.

Love, Jay x

11th April

Dear Diary,

Back to school today. I sat by the phone all night but he still hasn't rung. I think I've just got to admit it was nothing more than a holiday romance. He's never going to ring. He'll have another girl in tow by now, I bet... But what would happen if I'm out tonight catching up with Meg's holiday news, when he rings. Mum or Dad would find out everything! Or perhaps he'll just hang up rather than talk to them and I won't even know he's called. Meg did look jetlagged when I called for her this morning, so maybe she'll cancel our rendezvous herself.

Dave looked healthy enough this morning and I wondered whether he'd been ill at all. Mitzy came over to him in the schoolyard, and was hardly acting like she'd not seen him all week even though he told me that today was his first time out of the house. She was different with him. I couldn't quite put my finger on why exactly.

I felt a bit weird with him, even guilty about my snog with Pat and decided I'd prefer him not to know. I wonder what he'll be up to tonight while I'm getting my ear chewed off by Megan.

11th April

Dear Jane,

I'm so glad that you enjoyed your visit to Emily's and that your quest for a life is improving daily! Sounds like your kiss was a memorable experience. I wish I could say the same thing, but all I can remember about mine was that the boy in question tasted like an ashtray. (That was when smoking was fashionable.) Remember, my dear, that practice makes perfect, and always make sure you remove your chewing gum before you start. Oh, and another good idea is to ask them as casually as possible if they have ever had a cold sore. Catch them, and you'll suffer for years to come!

Love as always, Gran x

12th April

Dear Diary,

Meg and I had a brilliant time last night, and for the first time I was able to have a proper conversation with her about boys, rather than just nodding, agreeing and laughing in the right places as though I have some knowledge of the opposite sex. Now finally, I do! She told me that she had met a guy called Jeff. No matter how hard I try, I can't shake off this mental image I have of him wearing a stetson, cowboy boots and spurs!

Once she had paused for breath, I told her my news and made it sound as romantic and perfect as possible. That didn't take much doing really, but I purposely avoided telling her that he had promised to ring. He still hasn't and I'm doubting his word now. I asked Mum and Dad when I got back and they said no, the phone hadn't so much as rung the whole evening. Maybe he's lost my number. I'm considering asking Em to pass his number on to me.

Anyway, we were in the middle of all this when

Dave knocked. I was quite annoyed at his intrusion because he knew it was girls only for a change, but he was obviously only there because Mitzy must have been doing something else and he was probably bored on his own. I purposely avoided asking him where she was because it would have made me look interested then. Megan was pleased to see him and proceeded to tell him everything she had just told me. (She later told me that she was trying to get him to be jealous.)

When he had heard enough, he asked me about my trip. I played down the Patrick side of things, but Megan told him instead. I got really embarrassed but Dave was keen to hear more. I tried to tell him it was no big thing and he finally got the message that I wasn't going to tell him the details. Maybe this was some kind of revenge, making him feel the same way as we did when he sprung Mitzy on us. Maybe I should have gone into graphic detail to see whether he was jealous, but he went quiet anyway. I wondered if he was jealous, or had just had enough tales of love and romance?

me playing it cool!

I think that I might have to ring Pat myself, or would I look over enthusiastic, to the point of desperate? Maybe he is ill and can't get to a phone, or maybe he's just realised he made a mistake and doesn't want to know me now. But why would he have changed his mind so quickly? He said that he liked me and I don't think he was lying to me. Or maybe he was and he likes using girls. Ooh! Dilemma time. I'll ring Em tomorrow and ask her advice. She might have inside information for me by now. I'll have to know one way or another, because this is driving me insane!

13th April

Dear Jay,
 I have just been to see Patrick on your behalf. I asked him what he was playing at and he said that he hasn't rung you because it would have been leading you on. He doesn't think that long distance love affairs can ever work, no matter how much the two people are attracted to each other.
 I spoke to Gaby about it afterwards, and she said that he may be telling the truth, but there is more to it than that. I hate to be the one to tell you all this, Jay, but since you were down, he's got back with his girlfriend, Marigold. They split up about two months ago, but in a way, you helped them get back together because you made him realise that he still loved her. I was so annoyed with them both for not telling me sooner. You're better off without him, Jayne. I've seen him in a different light now. Please let me know that you're not completely devastated by this news, but I felt you finally deserved to hear the truth. Write soon so I don't worry unnecessarily about you.
 Love, Em x

Dear Diary,

I've just noticed the date is the thirteenth. How appropriate! I feel so *stupid*. How could he have used me like that? I must have looked such an easy target to him. I can't believe that I have wasted so much time thinking about him. At one point, I was even thinking about names for our children! To think that if I hadn't gone to visit, he might still be young free and single is no relief either. *Marigold*! I can just imagine what she looks like. Pretty, glamorous, popular, rich! What chance did I ever have? If he hadn't been on the rebound and desperate for affection, he wouldn't have looked twice at me. I have told *everyone* at school about him. They're all going to be asking me questions about him. It's so humiliating! My emotions have been on a roller coaster for the past few weeks now, and I think it's time to get off. Actually, I don't think I want to get on it again either. I can do without all this heartbreak. Boys are just trouble.

14th April

Dear Gran,

I just had to write and tell you that the man of my dreams turned out to be a rat. He was just using me and I feel totally stupid! I can't wait to see you. Actually, I've got a confession to make. I was considering postponing my visit to go and see him instead. Well, at least one good thing has come out of this. I have realised that I'm not ready for a

relationship yet and I am going to lead a life of
celibacy until I'm in university at least. From now
on, I am going to dedicate my life to my studies,
then that way I'm sure not to be hurt ever again. I
don't think I could stand feeling like this more than
once in one lifetime!

Write soon and cheer me up!

Love, Jayne x

17th April

Dear Em,

I know you asked me to reply swiftly, but I've
been busy thinking. First, thanks for telling me and
you can tell him that I'm glad he's back with his
girlfriend and that I haven't lost any sleep over him.
The truth is, the murderous and suicidal tendencies
have passed now and I am putting the whole thing
into perspective. I should have realised what he was
like when he wormed his way out of giving me his
phone number. Anyway, that is the last I'm going to
say on the matter. It really is all water under the
bridge now, so don't you go falling out with your
friends because of me. I want to be able to come and
visit again, and for things to be as though nothing
had ever happened.

Have you heard from Dave lately? I get the
feeling that all is not what it seems with him and
Mitzy. Has he told you anything? Has Megan bored
you with the stories of America and Jeff yet? Can
you imagine the size of the pieces Dave and I are
going to have to put together when this relationship

Patrick

108

falls apart too? After all, everyone knows long distance relationships can't work! You'd think she'd have learned her lesson after Jonathan. She should take a page out of my book and become a nun until she's at least twenty years old!

I'm thinking of arranging a little get together for her birthday. Would you be able to come down? Try to keep it a secret for now.

Love, Jay x

4th May

Dear Jane, sorry Jayne,

What a horrible boy you got yourself involved with. Who does he think he is upsetting you like that? Don't waste your time thinking about the 'What ifs'. Just think of the positive side – that your first kiss was enjoyable. You do know that you are too good for his type, don't you? There are plenty more fish in the sea, and don't let one bad experience put you off trying any more. Mr Right is still waiting for you.

How is David by the way? I think that now would be a good time to make your move on him. I agree that a good education is important, but you are only young once. Enjoy yourself while you can.

Love, Gran x

6th May

Dear Diary,

Gran was right. I've been consoling myself that my first snog was with a hunk! I am trying to think less about him but it's not working very well. I've decided to arrange a surprise party for Meg to keep my mind off boys, and that includes Dave.

Meg's mum has transformed the little gathering into a huge birthday bash, which isn't surprising because her family don't know the meaning of the word 'small'. I've been making loads of revision time for myself and I'm determined to do well. Even after what Gran said about Dave, I don't think I want to get involved again with anyone, especially when he probably doesn't like me that way. From now on, my heart will be unpenetrable.

Chapter 12

26th May

Dear Gran,

Last day of term again! It's brilliant how fast this year is going. It's Meg's surprise birthday party tomorrow and amazingly, Mum has given me a small rise in my pocket money so I can buy some new clothes. Em is coming down too, so I'll be able to tell you all about it when I see you. I'll ring you from the station. Can't wait to see you.

Love, Jayne x

27th May

Dear Diary,

I'm writing this on the train to Gran's. I can't believe I'm here alone. I am just such an adult these days!

We had a great night. It was my job to make sure Meg was out of the house all day and thankfully Em's arrival distracted her. She came close to smelling a rat when we had to take a detour to the Pizza Place via her house. I told her that she should tell her mum that she may be out late, and luckily she fell for this suggestion hook, line and sinker! She was totally taken in by the surprise. It took her ages to calm down! Em had a hoard of friends from school around her, Meg was doing an excellent impression of a startled bunny and social butterfly at the same time, so I found myself talking to Dave. Seconds later, Mitzy arrived and she beckoned him over to her. He looked at me as though to excuse himself, but I just picked up my coke and walked away. He's like a little puppy. She calls, he runs.

I had to go home early because of the obscene hour this train was leaving. I said goodbye to the birthday girl who was thrilled by the attention and told me that she was so grateful to me for suggesting it. I promised that I'd see Em in the summer holidays, which is only nine weeks away. I looked *everywhere* for Dave to say goodbye, but he was obviously busy with Mitzy. Things can't be as bad as I thought between them after all.

I doubt I'll be writing much this week. Who knows what Gran and I will be getting up to!

2nd June

Dear Diary,

I'm writing this while I am at my favourite place in the whole world – the beach at Gran's. It's her birthday today and almost by chance, we ended up here. It's cold and windy, but so peaceful. I love to come here and just think. Actually, I've done a lot of thinking (and eating and talking) since I got here and I've come to a few decisions.

1. I am going to be as sensible as possible around Mum and Dad. I want to show them that I am becoming a mature young woman, and I am grateful for the trust they are showing me these days.

2. I am going to do so well at school that they can't moan at me for anything.

3. I am going to stop being jealous of Meg. I have spent my whole life since I've known her wanting to be her, and it's time I realised that I won't ever be and should start to like myself more instead.

4. I am going to let Emily go. I have been desperately holding onto the thought that one day she might come back, and things will be the same as before. I've realised that, although we'll stay really good friends, I can't keep worrying that her new friends will become closer to her than me. As she sees them every day then they probably will. I have got to carry on making the effort to see her whenever I can.

5. I have also been considering the Dave situation. I have been in utter turmoil and it was only after talking everything through with Gran that she made me realise the reason things have been so strained between us is because I have been jealous. I am ready to admit that I never let Meg get near him, that I disliked Mitzy as soon as she started going out with him and that I have found it difficult to be around him at all because I like him, a lot! Now I have finally admitted that to myself, there only remains one problem. What can I do about it? Should I tell him? It might be less

stressful if he knew, but what would his reaction be? He's hardly going to finish with lovely, popular Zitzy to go out with me. Even if he did, my name would be dirt all over the school – *everybody* likes Mitzy. Maybe he would be horrified at the idea of the girl who he sees as a sister fancying him! He could reject me altogether then!

I think the best thing to do is wait. He and Zitzy seem to be having problems anyway, and I can wait a bit longer! Gran told me just to go home and tell him. She says that I've wasted enough time admitting all this to myself, but I'm still coming to terms with it! I'll just have to wait and see how brave I'm feeling on Monday morning.

4th June
Dear Diary,
   I've just got home and found this letter waiting for me.

2nd June

Dear Jay,
   Hope you had a lovely time at your gran's. Sorry I didn't see you for very long, but the summer's not too far away. Meg said she would love to come, but only after she gets back from the States. Act surprised when she tells you, but during the party, Jeff phoned her! He's invited her to stay over at his ranch! She was on cloud

114

nine, when Nick gave her a little birthday kiss that made her look twice at him. Dave later told her that Nick was completely in love with her and she asked me what she should do. I told her that he was lovely and said that it was just that she sees so much of him, she's been unable to really notice him before.

Talking of which, Dave was annoyed with you. He couldn't believe you'd gone away for a week without saying 'bye to him. I did defend your honour and said you had been looking for him when he was having his big heart to heart with Mitzy. As you know, I have no shame, so I asked him if everything was okay between them. He told me that they had just finished! He didn't want to talk about it, so it's your turn to find out the missing pieces of the jigsaw now!

Love, Em x

I am amazed! Maybe fate has decided to give me a break at last. I'm going to have to plan my strategies now.

4th June

Dear Gran,
You will not believe what has happened. Dave and Mitzy are no more! Where should I go from here? What should I say or do? Should I just act normal? What if that gives him time to think that he's made a mistake, and I lose him to his ex like I did with Patrick? Would Mitzy want him back though?

my head
is spinning!

115

There are loads of boys who are interested in her
and they'll be pleased to see her single again. This
is so amazing – it's as though my life is finally
falling into place at last. Missing you loads
already.

   Love, Jayne x

6th June

Dear Jane,

   Don't get ahead of yourself. Who broke it
off between them? Dave might be upset and
hurt and may need time to get over it.
Listen to your instincts and I'm sure you're
in for a wonderful time. I told you that
all things come to those who wait, didn't I?
   Enjoy yourself!
   Love, Gran x

7th June

Dear Diary,

   I was just unpacking when the door bell rang. It
was Meg. She said she'd come to thank me for the
party idea. She told me all about the vast number
of cards and presents she got and casually
mentioned Jeff's phone call. Then she told me
about Nick and how they had spent the whole
night dancing and said that although she knew
him, she'd seen him in a whole new light that
evening. I know the feeling well!

She eventually got round to telling me about the big showdown with Dave and Mitzy. Then she said, 'Do you think that maybe now you can make your move on him? I think you've waited long enough!'

She told me that she'd known how right we were for each other for ages now, and that if I didn't grab him quick, someone else would. She ordered me over to see him and find out all the gory details from him.

this is me
- in shock!

I am stunned! She and Em have known for ages! I can't believe they never said anything before now. Good grief! It must have looked so obvious to them, and I've been struggling on my own all this time! Well, here goes nothing. I am actually going to do it. EEK!

I'm back. After all the deep breathing exercises and cold sweats, he was out when I got to his house! I'm going to have to leave it now. That's if I don't change my mind in the meantime.

Chapter 13

8th June

Dear Diary,

The first day back has left me exhausted. We have been given our exam timetable already and there's only two weeks revision time left. The pursuit of Dave is going to have to wait until they are over – I can't concentrate on two things at once.

He seemed pleased to see me this morning and I asked for Meg's opinion on what he thinks about me. She thinks that Dave is in denial like I was! She also told me that her lust for him ceased to exist when she saw the way the two of us were together, and she knew that even though she wanted him (and I reckon she probably could have had him too) he was meant to be mine. She's keeping her distance from Nick more than I thought she would. She's usually talking marriage by now. Thankfully, her experience with Jonathan must have made her see the error of her ways.

I didn't mention Mitzy to Dave at all, but he must have guessed I knew. He asked me if I wanted to know why they'd split up and I said it was up to him. I came across as too blunt and knew as soon as I said it that I'd thrown another chance away! He said that it wasn't important

118

anyway, and skulked off. I've blown it, I can tell.
I've acted too casual all along.

15th June

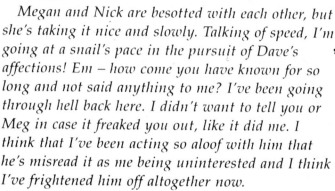

Dear Em,

Megan and Nick are besotted with each other, but she's taking it nice and slowly. Talking of speed, I'm going at a snail's pace in the pursuit of Dave's affections! Em – how come you have known for so long and not said anything to me? I've been going through hell back here. I didn't want to tell you or Meg in case it freaked you out, like it did me. I think that I've been acting so aloof with him that he's misread it as me being uninterested and I think I've frightened him off altogether now.

I should have a lot more time on my hands to concentrate on getting him after the exams. Did you know that we're having an end of term disco on the 15th July? Let me know if you can come so I can get you a ticket. Write soon.

Love, Jay x

18th June

Dear Jay,

I've known for ages about you and Dave, even before the thought entered your head I bet. I'm amazed it has taken you so long to realise you were meant for each other. The path of true love never runs smooth! It feels like I've been waiting for ever to talk to you about this!

I'm sorry, but I won't be able to come to the disco. We are having our end of term bash then too and I think I should try and get to know a few more people from school a bit better. I hope you don't mind too much.

It's brilliant news about Meg. Nick is so sweet and he's loved her for ages now. Ahh! It's just like you and Dave! Better sign off and let you get back to your revision!

Love, Em x

5th July

Dear Gran,

Hooray! I finished my very last exam this afternoon and without risking sounding too confident, I think I've done quite well. Meg, Nick, Dave and I are going out to celebrate tonight and the pursuit of Dave starts in earnest! Did I tell you that Meg told me to move fast too, because he won't be available soon – loads of girls apparently fancy him. Meg and Em have known about my little secret for ages too! As far as I know, he is available. Then again, I doubt he'd tell me if there was someone else after I showed so little interest in his love life with Mitzy.

Talking of Mitzy, I saw her talking to Jonathan today. They seemed rather pally.

Wish me luck for tonight.

Love, Jayne x

my dream

reality

7th July

Dear Diary,

So much for the rest of my life being plain sailing. Someone up there has really got it in for me.

We all went to the cinema and were stopped in our tracks. There were Mitzy and Jonathan – together! I just stood there in disbelief, but the expressions on poor Dave's and Meg's faces said it all. The timing couldn't have been better if they had planned it. Nick and I tried hard to bring some light relief to the gloomy atmosphere, but to no avail.

Meg said she was surprised to see Jonathan after he'd been making it up to her lately, but David said nothing, which was even more worrying. He must still like her. That would explain his moody behaviour. We are just never going to get together. I'm going to have to get a different life to the one I wanted.

10th July

Dear Diary,

Nothing much has happened the past week, until today. That is, excluding the fact that I'm convinced that David is avoiding me and that things between Meg and Nick are strained. This should be the best time of the year. We have finished all our work and we're spending most of the lessons doing nothing at all, and there's the disco to look forward to as well. Practically the whole school has bought tickets.

Mitzy came over to me to buy a couple earlier today and apologised for not seeing me since she and Dave split up. She said that she hasn't been avoiding me but did want to talk things over with me and asked if I would go for a milkshake with her after school. Reluctantly, I agreed. I never really wanted to talk to her about anything, but she was obviously under the impression that we are friends or something.

Before I knew where I was, we were drinking our shakes. We finally stopped the polite chit chat and she asked me if I'd been surprised to see her and Jonathan together. I said that it was none of my business, but she disagreed. She said that she couldn't explain it very well, but after Meg and Jonathan had the big show-down she had gone to see him to tell him how awful he'd been. Eventually, he thanked her, because she had been the only one of his friends with enough guts to stand up to him and tell him what they thought about him. He had finished with Phyllis because Mitzy had made him realise that he was using her too, just like he had done with Meg. Then she went on to say how, over the past few weeks, they'd got closer together.

While we were on the subject of men, I thought I'd mention David, and asked her why they'd split up. It felt strange talking to her about it, especially as I still hadn't got round to bringing the conversation up with him since last time. She sounded surprised and said, 'You mean he's not told you yet?' to which I replied no. Then she asked me if I'd not guessed and then finally said, "Jayne, he's in love with you. Always has been.'

I can't remember the rest of the conversation very well. I can't believe it! It's the best news I've ever had! I've got to tell Gran and Em straight away, then get over to Meg's. I'm bursting to let them know!

12th July

Dear Jane, sorry Jayne,
   I'm so pleased to hear your news. Isn't your gran always right? Let me know everything that happens!
   Love, Gran x

12th July

Dear Jay,
   HOORAY!! I'm so glad you finally know everything. I was hoping that Dave would tell you himself, but that's irrelevant now. What are you planning to do about it then? Let me know the plan of action and enjoy the disco!
   Love, Em x

Chapter 14

15th July

Dear Diary,

We broke up for seven weeks of heaven today! I got my exam results and I am a genius! Well, I could have got slightly better marks than I did, but still they were impressive enough for my mum and dad to promise me another rise in pocket money! Meg and Dave didn't do too badly either.

He still hasn't said anything to me and I can't bear to look him in the eye since I found out. In fact, I'm finding it hard to be in the same room with him and my heart races and my face flushes even when I hear his name mentioned!

I hope he says something in the disco tonight and with a bit of luck, I'll have some news to write up tomorrow.

15th/16th July

Dear Diary,

I have just ended the best night of my entire life. It's two o'clock in the morning and I am in bed, but there's no chance of me getting to sleep yet. I am too excited. I had better start at the beginning.

I got to the disco quite early with Megan because we were helping to sort everything out. The hall was starting to fill up when Mitzy and Jonathan came in. Meg's face went all red as Jonathan came over to her. I could tell she was dreading what he was about to say. He just said 'Sorry, Megan' and went away. We were flabbergasted. Mitzy just smiled.

We were just getting over the shock, when in came Nick and Dave. Meg almost ran over to Nick. She was making up for lost time with him. She said that she had treated him terribly over the week because of Jonathan putting her off men generally, but he had just restored her faith in the opposite sex.

Dave could see that I was on my own and he looked at me from across the room. I was about to smile at him, when he walked over to Mitzy instead. My heart sank and I almost started crying. Thankfully, Chris had noticed me on my own, and came over to ask me to dance. I was grateful for the distraction from a friend as my mind was working overtime wondering what on earth he could be saying to her. I decided there was no point letting him spoil the night I had been looking forward to for weeks, and was determined to enjoy myself no matter what.

Several songs later, I left Chris to get a drink. I looked around to see if Dave was still talking to Mitzy, but couldn't see either of them anywhere. Then, suddenly, I felt a tap on my shoulder. 'Who are you looking for?' I heard Dave say. 'You actually,' I replied, in the most casual voice I could manage. Then he asked me to dance.

As we were dancing, I kept getting the feeling that he was looking at me. It unnerved me slightly, but I thought I would look at him. He was just staring at me. Everything seemed to stop and then he took hold of my hand and led me off the dance floor and into a quiet corner.

My head was reeling and without either of us saying a word, he leaned over and kissed me! I still can't believe it! We never said anything about it until the dance music stopped and all the slow records came on. We went back to the dance floor in silence and for the first time in my life I was dancing to a slow record. (It was a lot easier than I had anticipated it to be too!!)

Finally, he said that he had been totally torn apart emotionally over what to do and had finally asked Mitzy for advice. She said she'd already told me and that she reckoned I was very keen too! It's a good thing she did because he would have been waiting forever for the right moment. Lucky for us Mitzy's an old romantic!

The rest of the night just flew by. We waved at Meg and Nick, who were smiling inanely at us, and on the way out we stopped by Mitzy and Jonathan. I just looked at them both and smiled

He held my hand so tightly all the way home. It felt strange in one way, but very right in another. It was as if I never knew him at all and my stomach was doing somersaults! We talked about how we had both been feeling, how strange it had been when we had noticed our feelings changing, how we had disliked the other having boy/girlfriends but couldn't work out why until we realised we were jealous. He told me how furious he had been when Meg had told him that I had kissed Patrick but how he had tried so hard to keep it hidden. I told him about how devastated I was to see him holding hands with Mitzy for the first time.

Suddenly, we found ourselves on my doorstep. I could have spent the whole night just kissing him there but I was convinced I saw the curtains twitch in Vicky's room. He is a brilliant kisser. I thought Pat's was nice but it was so much nicer with Dave. Gran said practice makes perfect and I'm not going to mind practising!

I'll have to turn in now. I don't think I'll get a wink of sleep tonight though. Wonder if he will?

17th July

Dear Gran,

It has finally happened. David and I are at last an item. And it was definitely worth the wait and the heartbreak. I can't wait to see you next week to tell you all about it.

We are going to visit Emily first. Meg is taking Nick, and of course, Dave is coming too. Mum was a bit wary now that she knows he is my boyfriend, but she said that she trusts me to be sensible! Isn't that amazing? She is treating me more like a young adult now.

Megan has decided not to go to America after all because she has realised that it was a holiday

romance, and that she would be furious if Nick was
considering doing the same thing.

This is going to be the best summer yet.

Love, Jayne xx

19th July

Dear Jane, sorry Jayne,

You can't imagine how pleased I am to
hear about you and Dave. Is there any
chance of him joining you when you come to
visit? I hope you all have a wonderful
break from school, and now that you have
got the life you were so desperately looking
for, enjoy it thoroughly – but this is just
the beginning.

Love as always,

Gran x